This book should be return
Lancashire County Library or

2 0 SEP 2016

3 0 OCT 2017

23 DEC 2017

A YEAR IN THE LIFE OF A TOTAL AND COMPLETE GENIUS

STACEY MATSON

ANDERSEN PRESS • LONDON

First published in Great Britain in 2015 by
Andersen Press Limited
20 Vauxhall Bridge Road
London SW1V 2SA
www.andersenpress.co.uk

2 4 6 8 10 9 7 5 3 1

First published in 2014 in Canada by Scholastic Canada Limited

British Library Cataloguing in Publication Data available.

ISBN 978 1 78344 301 7

Printed and bound in Great Britain by
Clays Ltd, St Ives plc

For Mom and Dad

OCTOBER

The Next Great Canadian Novel
(Title to be announced)

By Arthur Bean

~~Once upon a time there was~~

~~There was once a~~

~~A long time ago~~

~~Yesterday~~

~~Today~~

~~America is awesome! This is because~~

~~The USA is nothing like Canada~~

~~A boy and his unicorn sat on the grass and the unicorn could talk and said~~

~~Murder! There's been a very violent murder!~~

Dear Ms Whitehead,

As you know, I haven't been in class yet, but my next door neighbour Nicole suggested that I write you a letter since I will be starting soon. I don't really know what to write to you. Maybe I will tell you a little about myself so that you feel like I started school at the same time as everyone else.

My name is Arthur Aaron Bean, but I normally just go by Arthur. I spent the summer at my grandparents' house in Balzac. It was a long summer. I actually live in one of the apartment buildings pretty close to the school. I like to knit and watch movies, sometimes at the same time. I'm a very good multi-tasker. I like creative writing, so I hope that we will do that and that I didn't miss it. I was probably the best writer in my elementary school, and I plan on getting rich as a novelist when I'm a grown-up. I don't have any siblings, but my cousin Luke is kind of like my twin brother.

My most profound work so far is the heartwarming story called "Sockland." In this short story, a little boy climbs into the dryer during a game of hide-and-seek with his older brothers. He is accidentally shrunk and crawls through the dryer vent into Sockland. Sockland is a land where missing socks go to live. He enjoys it for a while, but then finds that single socks are very boring, and needs to find a way to get home. He then gets the socks to help him by promising to send their partners through the tunnel, and he crawls back up into the dryer to rejoin humanland. Mrs. Lewis said it was highly original and that I showed real promise of becoming the next J.K. Rowling.

The secretary told me that I'm in a class with some of the people from my elementary school so that I would feel more comfortable. Actually, she didn't say people, she said some of my friends. This seems weird, because I wasn't really friends with a lot of the people in my elementary school. Actually, most of my friends went to the Catholic school next door to our school, and so I saw them all the time. I did have a couple of friends like Oliver, but mostly I wasn't friends with people in my elementary school class. Besides, who would want to be friends with guys like Robbie Zack? I'm not friends with people who spell thoughts as thots. Good luck with that one. He's what my mother called "a handful of trouble with a capital T."

Yours truly,
Arthur Bean

Dear Arthur,

Thank you for your letter, and welcome to Terry Fox Junior High! I'm so pleased to welcome you to both my homeroom and my English class! I was also sorry to hear about the sad circumstances that delayed your start of grade seven. Please know that I am available to discuss anything with you anytime you may need.

I'm so pleased that you will be in my class. I hope we can explore and create some wonderful and imaginative spaces together this year. Since you've painted such a good picture of yourself, here are a few things I'll share with you so that we can get to know each other!

In my spare time (when I'm not marking homework) I like to canoe, cross-country ski and take my dog Bruno for walks. My favourite book is The Grapes of Wrath by John Steinbeck, and my favourite play is A Midsummer Night's Dream by Shakespeare. I hope that it will soon be your favourite play also, since we'll be studying it this winter!

I'm glad that creative writing excites you, and it sounds like you are ready to challenge yourself in my class. I look forward to reading some of your work and I hope to learn more about your hobbies as the year progresses.

One more note: Please be respectful of your classmates. Everyone has different strengths, and bad spelling doesn't mean that someone is not creative. Agatha Christie was a terrible speller and look how famous her books are!

Ms Whitehead

Dear Ms Whitehead,

Who is Agatha Christie?

Yours truly,
Arthur Bean

▸▸ ▸▸ ▸▸

ATTENTION: ALL FUTURE AUTHORS!
Terry Fox Junior High is pleased to be participating
in a city-wide Junior Authors Short Story Contest.
Winners of the contest will be published in a
national Junior Authors issue of *Writers Write
Now (WWN)* magazine. You can also win $200!
Deadline for Stories: April 1st
Watch this board for more details!

▸▸ ▸▸ ▸▸

Assignment: Personal Letters
Write a letter to your future self. The time is up to you: you can
write to yourself at the end of this school year, when you are
graduating high school, when you get married or maybe when
you are retiring! Imagine what your life will be like, and ask
yourself some questions. Be sure to tell yourself about your life
now too! Please ensure that you use the proper letter structure
we covered in class.

Due: October 8

▸▸ ▸▸ ▸▸

October 8

Arthur Bean
Apt. 16, 155 Tormy Street
Calgary, AB

A.A. Bean
1 Park Avenue
Penthouse
New York, NY

Dear Future Arthur,

Hello. How are you? I am fine, thank you for asking.
I was surprised to find out that you live in New York,
although a penthouse on Park Avenue sounds nice.
It's one of the most expensive places in Monopoly, so
you must be very famous and very rich. Does your
cousin Luke still live next door? It's so nice that you
guys get to share a pool and see each other every day.
How is your wife, Kennedy? It seems so funny to me
to think that it was only this year that you met this
blonde goddess. Remember how you saw her every
day in class and never said anything to her, but then
you asked her to dance at the Halloween Dance? It
was so nice the way she fainted in your arms and you
were so manly, picking her up and carrying her out of
the dance. From then on, she called you her prince.
Does she still call you Prince Arthur? I can't wait
until this actually happens, since it's only October
here. I bet the Halloween Dance was the same night
Robbie Zack got rabies and died. May he rest in peace.
How is your most recent famous novel coming along?
I only just started part one of our autobiography, and
I am still working on the greatest novel ever. Plus,
now I'm starting a story to win the story competition,
but of course you know that because you won it!
I'm so glad you were able to finish it *and* your novel

in one year, and then write forty-five more books. Which book did you sell to become a movie first? I hope it was a good one. In case you were wondering about me, I guess things are OK. Pickles has run away again. She was a terrible cat anyway, and her hair was falling out. I think she is sad. Or maybe she ran off with the tabby two doors down to start a new cat family. Whatever. I have almost finished knitting my first sweater. Nicole from next door says that my stitches are very even. I hope it's finished by the time it's cold outside, which might be tomorrow. HAHAHA. My next project will be a sweater for Pickles if she ever comes back. Please tell Kennedy that I love her, and write back soon. HAHAHA.

Sincerely,
Arthur Bean

▶▶ ▶▶ ▶▶

Arthur,

Your letter flows well from one topic to another, and you've done a nice job of creating a new world for your famous self! Remember to use different paragraphs for different ideas; this will help to separate and organize your letter. Your use of humour is great; however, please (again) refrain from killing off your classmates. Respect goes a long way.

Ms Whitehead

▶▶ ▶▶ ▶▶

Ongoing Reading Journal

As we move through the year, we will be reading and discussing books in class and in small groups. I would like you to keep track of your thoughts about these books and other books you read this year in an ongoing reading journal. You may want to write about how the book made you feel, what you like or do not like about the book, or what the book means to you. Feel free to write about any books you read in your journal; this is *your* space! I will be marking these with a participation mark, meaning that you will not be judged on your writing style or your feelings about the books, but on how you respond to the work overall. Hopefully writing down your thoughts about what you read will elevate the in-class conversations.

October 12th

Dear Reading Journal,

Do you mind if I call you RJ? I've always wanted to have a friend who only goes by his initials. There was a kid named PJ in my elementary school, but he wasn't very nice to me. He used to hang out with Robbie Zack, and together they would pick on kids who were smaller than them. It's not my fault that I'm short. PJ used to laugh when Robbie Zack would put mouldy sandwiches in my gym bag every morning after the bell rang. Robbie would tell people that I smelled like farts because my last name was Bean. But I smelled like farts because he put mouldy food in my backpack. Like I try and tell my dad, it ain't easy being Bean.

So I think maybe Robbie is like the jerk kids in *Word Nerd*. Or maybe like the whole school in *The Chocolate War*. Although Robbie never beat me up, so I guess it's not as bad as in those books.

Speaking of books, I thought *Word Nerd* was good, but *The Chocolate War* was boring, and I didn't get the ending. Did the guy die? I can't tell. Anyway, RJ, I've been reading a lot of books because I am a writer too. In fact, there's a writing competition at school and I'm going to win it. Good night, RJ.

Yours truly,
Arthur Bean

▶▶ ▶▶ ▶▶

Assignment: Elegies and Odes

Write an elegy or an ode like the ones we studied in class. Your poem must be at least three stanzas long. Perhaps you would like to write a funny elegy (maybe about the death of your favourite pair of shoes) or an inspirational ode. Have fun with it!

A quick review:

An ode is a poem that compliments someone or something that inspires the poet.

An elegy is a mournful or sad poem, usually written as a funeral song or a lament for the dead.

Due: October 14

▶▶ ▶▶ ▶▶

Elegy for Bobby Mack, a totally made-up bully who is not based on any person in my real life

By Arthur Bean

Your father's football jacket
That never fit you anyway
Lies empty on your floor
Since I doubt you put your clothes in the closet

What an embarrassing thing
To die like Elvis did
But not to be famous
So it's not even cool

Your dreams of working
The night shift at McDonalds
Were flushed down the toilet
That night

I'm sure Tyler and Richie
Will miss you on the bus
But I will not, since I could smell you
And I sat three seats ahead of you

Never again will I be forced to listen
To your dumb, stupid insults
About my knitting and my looks
Both of which are cool, by the way

Your voice, once louder and
More obnoxious than 1000 screaming chimps
Will yell stupidities no more
The world breathes a sigh of relief.

Arthur, please see me after class.

Ms Whitehead

An Ode to Knitting

By Arthur Bean

Oh the sound of the needles
Clicking and clacking away
They sound like a pair of beetles
Mating on a pile of hay

My sweater is practically finished
There's only one arm left to do
But I've run out of wool that will match
Don't think that I feel diminished
I'll just knit in a few rows of blue
And hope that my new fad will catch

Most people say that it's geeky
That a boy who makes sweaters should quit
But that's when I say something cheeky:
I tell them, "It takes balls to knit!"

Arthur, this is much better use of your
talents! A good use of humour and
rhyming; a proper ode to your unique
hobby!

Ms Whitehead

►► ►► ►►

October 15th

Dear RJ,

Today I was reading a book in class, but I don't
really remember anything I read. This is for
two reasons. One reason is because the book
was dumb and seemed to involve cowboys and
horses, which seems very outdated since no one
is really a cowboy anymore. The second reason
has to do with class. Ms Whitehead decided to
pair us up for the creative writing contest. She
said that it would be good to have a "second
set of eyes" for our work. I pointed out that the
people who wear glasses already have a second
set of eyes, but apparently that's "impertinent."
Anyway, you'll never guess who my partner is,
RJ . . . it's Kennedy! Kennedy Laurel is going to
be my partner for creative writing. This will be
difficult, I think, since I want to be supportive of
her work, but I also want to win the competition.
I'm so glad that we're paired with kids from other
classes. It makes it more professional. I mean, I
would hate to have her see my work in class and
be intimidated by how good it is. I bet her story
is a love story. I heard from Oliver yesterday that
Kennedy has a boyfriend, AND he's in grade
eight. So her story will be all kisses and true
love, which is total crap. My story will be way
better. I still think she's awesome, so I hope she's
not too sad when she comes in second.

    I think that I'm supposed to say something
here about the book I'm reading too — I'm not
really sure. It's a book for class. It's OK, because
the author is pretty good about explaining how

it feels when your mom is gone. It's like my life is the same as the dumb cowboy in the book who is not crying. Except I'm not a cowboy, and I'm definitely not going to be crying after I win $200. So now all I need is the greatest idea ever for the greatest story ever. Not like it will take me long to do that.

Yours truly,
Arthur Bean

▶▶ ▶▶ ▶▶

From: Kennedy Laurel (imsocutekl@hotmail.com)
To: Arthur Bean (arthuraaronbean@gmail.com)
Sent: October 23, 9:21

Hi Arthur! I'm really excited that you are my creative writing partner!!! LOL!! I LOVE writing stories, and it's gonna be really fun sharing ideas with you! I didn't even know you liked writing! You should join the newspaper! We have a lot of fun reporting on stuff! And it's GREAT practice for writing!

So far, I think my story for the contest is going to be a VAMPIRE story! It will be something about a guy who is locked in a mental institution because he sees VAMPIRES and keeps telling people that they are coming for him, but people think he's crazy. Of course, the vamps will be real LOL! I'm not sure how it will end yet, but probably something GORY! Do you have any ideas?!

Kennedy ☺

From: Arthur Bean (arthuraaronbean@gmail.com)
To: Kennedy Laurel (imsocutekl@hotmail.com)
Sent: October 23, 10:04

Dear Kennedy,

I love you

From: Arthur Bean (arthuraaronbean@gmail.com)
To: Kennedy Laurel (imsocutekl@hotmail.com)
Sent: October 23, 10:09

Sorry, Kennedy! I accidentally hit send before finishing that sentence. I meant to say I love your idea! I don't know how your story should end, but I will think about it. I also will join the newspaper with you. That sounds good. I'm not sure how much time I will be able to spend on it, since I write a lot already. I plan on becoming a world famous author, so I need to practise. I think my story will be an epic story. I've been thinking that maybe it will be the story of a poor man who thinks he's a knight. He lives in a village and thinks that windmills are dragons, so he tries to kill them. It sounds funny, but it will be very sad. He will think that a peasant in the next village is a princess for him to save. At the end, he will die of heartbreak. That's sort of the main storyline so far.

Yours truly,
Arthur Bean

From: Kennedy Laurel (imsocutekl@hotmail.com)
To: Arthur Bean (arthuraaronbean@gmail.com)
Sent: October 23, 20:13

Hi Arthur! You are SO funny! I'm glad you are going to join the newspaper! That will make TWO new reporters LOL! Robbie Z is also going to join! Do you know Robbie? We are next door neighbours! Well, not quite, but he lives across the street and we've been playing baseball on the same team SINCE T-BALL! I know Robbie hates writing, but we ALWAYS need photographers and artists LOL!

Anyways, your story sounds pretty good, but . . . um . . . I'm pretty sure that there's a famous story like that already? My parents took me to a play called *Man of La Mancha* and it was kind of the same as your story! Maybe you saw the same play and forgot that you saw it LOL! That happens to me all the time too LOL! I bet you could change it though, and make it a new story! LOTS of GREAT writers rewrite other stories!

Anyways, have a good weekend and I will see you at the newspaper meeting on Monday at lunch! Room 204! My boyfriend is taking me BOWLING tomorrow LOL! TOO funny LOL!

Kennedy ☺

October 24th

Dear RJ,

We're still reading the cowboy book. I don't actually know why we're studying it. I mean, Ms Whitehead said that SHE studied it in junior high. How old is this book?! And why do authors write stories based in "reality"? It's lame. First, like I said before, cowboys aren't really real, not the way books describe them. And no kid would ever call himself a cowboy. That's like kids who play D&D calling themselves geeks. *Cowboys Don't Cry*? Of course they don't. Who would "identify" with this book? I bet Ms Whitehead would say that it's "symbolic." My mom told me that symbolism in books was all made up, but I think that the ranch in this book symbolizes boredom for everybody who has to read it. Luke said that his class is reading *The Hunger Games*. That sounds way better. I wish we lived close by him and then I would get to read better books in school.

I would rather read a story where the world isn't real, where the world is made up, with ogres and knights and magic. At least then the good guys are good guys, and the princess doesn't have a next door neighbour who is a guy who "accidentally" hits people on the head with his backpack on his way to the back of the bus the way Robbie does to me. She also doesn't have a boyfriend in grade eight who takes her bowling. Who goes bowling anyway? My story for the competition is going to take place in a different world. I can already describe what all the monsters look like. It's going to be awesome, and all the judges are going to be amazed at how I was able to create a whole new world and paint images inside their minds.

In my story, I won't kill off the parents either, because it sucks for the kid who reads that book and knows what it feels like when his mom dies, and it sucks for everybody else who has to be in a class with a kid whose mom has died and then they look at him to answer all the questions the teacher asks about how the character is feeling.

Yours truly,
Arthur Bean

▶▶ ▶▶ ▶▶

From: Kennedy Laurel (imsocutekl@hotmail.com)
To: Arthur Bean (arthuraaronbean@gmail.com)
Sent: October 25, 21:10

Hi Arthur! I didn't see you at the newspaper meeting at lunch today! Then I thought that maybe I forgot to tell you what room it was in LOL! For next time, it's in Mr. Everett's lab! Mr. E. is SUCH a nerd but he's funny LOL! ANYWAYS, I signed you up to do an article on the Halloween Dance! I can't wait to see your costume! Also, have you thought more about your story? I think that maybe in mine one of the nurses will be an ALIEN! Crazy twist LOL!

Kennedy ☺

▶▶ ▶▶ ▶▶

Assignment: Acrostic Poems

Write an acrostic poem about a person in your life. It could be a poem about your dog, your boyfriend/girlfriend, your grandmother, or maybe even a poem about a celebrity you find inspiring. A reminder: an acrostic poem uses the first letter of a word or name at the beginning of each line. Extra points if your poem rhymes!

Due: October 26

My Dad

By Arthur Bean

Every night, he sits in a chair
Reality shows on the TV blare
Not watching them really
Each one looks so silly
Sometimes he smiles weakly
To me it looks meekly
But he's there every night
Ernest Bean will be alright
As long as he's not dumb, and
Never forgets my mom.

Dear Arthur,

Your acrostic is a lovely ode to your father, but it's quite sad. Maybe next time you can try focusing on his best qualities or your favourite memories that include him. It might make you feel better. Did he teach you to ride a bicycle? Does he play catch with you in *the backyard? This is a real departure from the humour in your previous work. Know that you can speak to me privately should you be encountering any problems at school or at home.*

Ms Whitehead

From: Kennedy Laurel (imsocutekl@hotmail.com)
To: Arthur Bean (arthuraaronbean@gmail.com)
Sent: October 26, 17:04

Hi Arthur! Did you get my message about the newspaper and the article about the Halloween Dance? I never heard back from you! The dance is on Friday night, I HOPE you can make it! I still don't have a costume! My bf wants to go as Fred and Wilma from the FLINTSTONES LOL! I told him that was crazy since I have BLONDE hair, not red LOL! Now I think we will go as a fisherman and a mermaid LOL! Anyway, Mr. Everett wants to have a first draft of your story at the newspaper meeting on MONDAY at NOON. Don't worry if it's not perfect (OF COURSE it's yours, so it probably will be anyway LOL) cuz Mr. E. edits everything anyway. He said that even HE makes spelling mistakes LOL! OK, I'm off to do some homework!

Kennedy ☺

From: Arthur Bean (arthuraaronbean@gmail.com)
To: Kennedy Laurel (imsocutekl@hotmail.com)
Sent: October 26, 17:20

Dear Kennedy,

Sorry I didn't make it to the meeting. I wasn't sure I wanted to join anymore but you convinced me. I'm very busy with my writing, because I'm working on a novel outside of school. I'm going to be the youngest winner of the Governor General's Award, but I need to write a lot. But since you seem so excited about it, I will be at the dance. I think I will go as a reporter. Funny, huh?
    See you on Friday. I'm sure it will be fun.

Yours truly,
Arthur Bean

From: Kennedy Laurel (imsocutekl@hotmail.com)
To: Arthur Bean (arthuraaronbean@gmail.com)
Sent: October 26, 19:06

Hooray!!! LOVE the costume idea LOLOLOL!!! And I CAN'T WAIT to read your PRIZE-WINNING NOVEL LOLOLOL!!!

Kennedy ☺

▶▶ ▶▶ ▶▶

Halloween Dance a Scream

By Arthur Bean

Terry Fox Junior High had a howl of a good time on Friday night at the Halloween Dance.

Taking first prize in the couples' costume contest were Amanda Lawrence and Jeffrey Wong for their inspired Romeo and Ghouliet costumes. Placing a close second were Kennedy Laurel and Sandy Dickason as Fisherman and Mermaid. Their second-place finish is likely because Kennedy's mermaid costume clearly outdid her boyfriend's flannel shirt and rubber boots. That's just pretending to be in costume. Everyone thought that Oliver Keith's Quasimodo would win Best Individual Costume, but he lost to Peter Lee's Couch Potato costume. I have a "hunch" Quasimodo will be "back" next year.

The party really started when the vampire DJ went on his coffin break, and the mummy DJ started spinning wrap music.

The most shocking event of the night was when Robbie Zack, dressed as a cannibal, was suspended from school. He was found in the Home Ec room, buttering up the teacher.

Hiya, Arthur,

A punster, like myself! What a great start on your first article. I'm going to look it over and make some edits in time for publication on Friday. For your next article, try to focus on finding the story, and not just the puns. And don't forget to stick to the truth and nothing but the truth. I appreciate the humour, but

we don't want to confuse our readers
by printing a photo of Robbie Zack
as Batman and referring to him as a
cannibal. (Wouldn't that be a new twist
in the next Batman comic?) Very funny,
though! Cheers!

Mr. Everett

P.S.: Why did the monster eat a light
bulb? She wanted a light snack!

NOVEMBER

Assignment: Call and Response Poems

In Friday's class, many of you commented on the lyrical qualities of the call and response poems. Sometimes we can find inspiration in the words of our colleagues, so I have assigned you a partner and would like you to write four to six stanzas of a "call and response" poem. In this poem, the first person (Person A) writes the first stanza. Then Person B will write a stanza that responds to Person A's writing. Person A will then respond to Person B and so forth. You may find yourselves surprised at what wonders collaboration can create!

Due: End of class today! (November 1)

Call and Response Poem

By Arthur Bean and Robbie Zack

(Robbie)
Poettry is for loosers
Sports are way more cool
Like hockey and bassketball
And even baseball is beter than a pome

(Arthur)
Your lack of intelligence astounds me
But then, your mean streak does too
Sports are for idiots, jerks and bullies
In short, they're for people like you

23

(Robbie)
There not for jerks, nerdball
There for people with skills like stick handleing
And running fast
Leaving loosers in dust
Where you will be

(Arthur)
I know you think you're cool
Cuz you're bigger than kids like me
But I will be famous, and you will be dumb
In the future, you just wait and see

(Robbie)
whatever.
your not worth my time
i just want to rite about sports

(Arthur)
You're confusing your you're with your your
Something we learned in grade three
But I guess to you grammar doesn't matter
Cuz it's not needed when you work at McD's

▶▶ ▶▶ ▶▶

November 3

Dear Ernest,

Your son Arthur is in my Language Arts and Creative Writing class. He is bright, enthusiastic and participates often in class discussions. However, I have some concerns about his behaviour, particularly concerning his interactions with one of his classmates, Robert Zack. I am worried about his aggression towards Robert and the disdain he shows for Robert's work. Robert is a student who struggles in the Language Arts setting, and I believe that it might be a great help to both Arthur and Robert to work together.

I'm proposing that Arthur become Robert's tutor for the next few months. I feel that Robert could certainly benefit from Arthur's knowledge and passion for the English language, and it may help Arthur to become more understanding of other people's foibles and challenges. I understand that Arthur and Robert have had some confrontations in the past, and I hope that some structured time one-on-one will help them interact on a more positive basis. The Terry Fox Junior High peer tutoring process takes place for one hour each week, directly after school, on an afternoon that is mutually convenient for the tutor and tutee. With your consent, I will set up a time to meet with Robert and Arthur to discuss the tutoring process.

Should you have any questions, please don't hesitate to contact me.

Sincerely,
Alexa Whitehead

Dear Ms Whitehead,

I would like to point out that my father is very strict about people referring to him as Ernest. He won't like you being so personal by using his first name instead of Mr. Bean. Secondly, I am very busy after school. I have activities on every evening, and I have writing to do for the school competition AND the newspaper. I don't think I could make it work with my very busy extracurricular schedule. I think you should reconsider sending this letter to my dad at all. He's a very busy man, and he is also very sad about losing his wife, so if he thinks his son is bad, it might break his heart and leave me an orphan. Don't you think I've been through enough?

Yours truly,
Arthur Bean

Arthur,

Please keep this revised letter in this <u>sealed</u> envelope for delivery to your father.

Thank you,
Ms Whitehead

▶▶　▶▶　▶▶

November 4th

Dear RJ,

I know that I'm supposed to use you for reading
responses, so I'm responding to a letter that
Ms Whitehead wrote to my father. It sucks.
It's the stupidest letter I've ever seen, and the
stupidest idea ever. For one thing, I think Robbie
will just use the time for tutoring to spit on my
paper. He used to do that in grade five when we
sat across from each other. Then I got in trouble
for handing in wet Math problems, and the cool
girls called me Droolyface. Not only that, but
Robbie is clearly stupid. My mom used to say
that calling people stupid is the worst thing you
can do, but I think that's stupid. Sorry, Mom.
Some people are stupid. People like Robbie Zack,
and people like Ms Whitehead for coming up
with some crappy punishment for me because
she knows I'm probably smarter than she is and
that I'm going to be famous and never dedicate a
book to her. I won't even thank her in the Thank
You section. All this tutoring is going to get in
the way of my writing time too. My story for the
competition is going to be way shorter now.
    Anyway, RJ, I just wanted to tell you this
because no one else will listen. If ever you want
to tell me something, RJ, I'll listen. HAHAHA.

Yours truly,
Arthur Bean

November 4th

Dear Mr. Everett,

I've been thinking a lot about my place in the Newspaper Club, and I would like to write a column once a month. In my article, I will comment on goings-on at school and in the world as I see them. I promise it will be funny, especially since I am practising to be a famous author one day.

Yours truly,
Arthur Bean

Hiya, Arthur,

Your suggestion for a running article is an interesting one! What enthusiasm and initiative for the newspaper! We normally reserve opinion pieces for the editors who have a couple of years of hard-hitting journalism in grades seven and eight behind them. Why don't you cover the Remembrance Day Assembly instead? We can see how that goes, along with a few other articles in the next couple of months and perhaps try a sample of a running article after a few more editions.

Cheers!
Mr. E.

▶▶ ▶▶ ▶▶

November 5th

Dear Alexa,

Please consider this letter as consent for Arthur to participate in the tutoring program. I'm glad he's able to help out.

Ernie B.

▶▶ ▶▶ ▶▶

November 7th

Dear RJ,

I have to start tutoring Robbie this Tuesday. I tried to talk to my dad, but he says I have to do it if my teacher thinks it's a good idea. He told me to "take it as a compliment." I don't know how spending time with a jerk is a compliment. I was talking to Luke about it today, and he said that I should say that I'm sick and go home early, and then when Ms Whitehead asks me about it, I could say that looking at Robbie's face makes me want to throw up. I thought that was pretty funny, don't you, RJ? Too bad Luke isn't around more often. We got to see them at Thanksgiving, but now I have to wait until Christmas. Talking to him on the phone sucks too. His mom always takes the phone from him and coos about sending her love. It's so lame.

Oh yeah. About reading books, Luke told me to read *Feed*, by M.T. Anderson. He said it's crazy-weird and funny so far. I'm going to see if the library has it tomorrow.

Anyway, wish me luck this week, RJ. I'm going to need it!

Yours truly,
Arthur Bean

▶▶ ▶▶ ▶▶

Peer Tutoring Program — Progress Report
Session: November 9th
Worked On: Synonyms

I think this is impossible. This guy is a turd.
— Arthur

I *concur* (agree)
— Robbie

▶▶ ▶▶ ▶▶

Assignment: Remembrance Day Poems
Write a poem for Remembrance Day. Look at some of the poems
we read and studied in class for inspiration. Perhaps your poem
is inspirational, or perhaps it is anti-war. Maybe you want to
consider writing the poetic story of a soldier in WWII. We'll
read the works in class and choose a favourite to be read at the
school Remembrance Day Assembly.

Due: November 10

War

By Arthur Bean

In schoolyard fields
The insults are said
Between the bullies
Grade to grade
They don't throw bombs
They throw water balloons
They think they're funny
They're just baboons
We are the nerds
Short days ago, we knit,
Felt pride, wrote songs
And poems, then felt wronged
And now we hide
In classrooms, side by side
Away from schoolyard fields
We are the lowest of the low
To cooler kids we throw
The answers to next week's test
And maybe they won't pick on us
At least until we miss the bus
And have to wait
In schoolyard fields

Dear Arthur,

Your re-imagined poem of "In Flanders Fields" is very interesting. I appreciate your creative variation on the assignment — to suggest that war could be considered bullying on a much larger scale. It is an intriguing concept. However, you understand that your liberal interpretation of the assignment would be inappropriate for a school assembly marking an occasion as solemn as Remembrance Day, don't you? Many people have a soft spot for this particular poem, even today.

Ms Whitehead

▶▶ ▶▶ ▶▶

We Shall Grow Old During the Assembly

By Arthur Bean

Terry Fox Jr. High celebrated another Remembrance Day with an assembly on November 10th. As expected from an assembly, there was the usual singing of the national anthem, a bad rendition of a mournful song by the choir, and some speakers. Three poems were read, one by a student in each grade. Representing the grade nines was Mikayla Connors, reading a rhyming poem pretending she was a dead soldier from World War I. Grade eight student Brianna Lau read her poem about being a dead soldier from World War II, and finishing off the trio was grade seven student Paige Petrovych, who read — yes, you got it — her poem about being a soldier who watches his best friend die in World War I. Certainly there were better poems in the grade seven class than this overwrought free verse. In case you fell asleep during this part of the show, you can read all three poems on page 5 of this edition of the Terry Fox Jr. High *Marathon*.

The poems were followed by the obligatory two minutes of silence, one of which was punctuated by a teacher's cell phone ringing. Read more about the school cell phone policy on page 1.

The best part of the assembly was the talk from a soldier who recently served in Afghanistan. Lt. Ducharme was funny but also serious, and told us some great and sad stories about life as a soldier and about living in a war zone. He should come to every assembly.

Hiya, Arthur,

There's some great work in your writing here! You've covered some of the major points of the assembly, and I like how you refer your readers to other parts of the newspaper. For your next piece, focus on being more objective while you are reporting. It's awesome that you covered everything so completely, so now try and look at your subject like a scientist! Think objectively, and avoid adding your own personal commentary. I've done some editing on your article to show you what I mean — check it out!

Would you like to try covering a school sporting event next? The boys' volleyball finals are next week. Should be a smashing game!

Cheers!
Mr. E.

Dear Mr. Everett,

No offence, but sports don't interest me. What I would really like is to write my own opinion pieces, since you've said that my voice is so strong. How about I write one article for the December edition of the paper, and you can review it beforehand? I'll have an article for you by the end of the week!

Yours truly,
Arthur Bean

Hiya, Arthur,

I think I'd like to see more articles from you before we look into a new format. After all, I'm still learning about the best format for the school paper too! The trials of being a first-year teacher! Could you review the short film that the AV Club made this fall? They will be showing it every lunch hour during the first week of December in the Drama room, but are willing to do a preview for the newspaper. I bet it leaves you reeling!

Cheers!
Mr. E.

▶▶ ▶▶ ▶▶

November 15th

Dear RJ,

I knew that the first month back at school
would be hard and stuff, but I didn't think it
was going to stay that way! First off, Luke was
right about there being so much homework.
I'm *always* doing homework, when what I
really want to work on is my short story for
the competition. I heard about this book that
teaches you how to write a novel in three days,
so I'm going to find that. I hope it has lots of
ideas to choose from. Can you imagine? If this
book tells you how to write a book in three
days, then it must take like an hour to write
a short story! I'm going to write something
like *Feed*. Luke was right. That book is super
weird and crazy, but it kind of feels like it could
actually happen in the future.

I still can't believe Ms Whitehead is
making me work with Robbie every week.
It's so terrible! He never does anything,
and he doesn't listen to me when I try to
do what we're told to do. He just sits there
and doodles on his page. They aren't even
doodles. He does these crazy drawings in his
margins. They are super elaborate and kind
of gruesome. Maybe if he wrote instead of
drew, we wouldn't have to meet every week.
Maybe I'll tell him that . . .

Oh, Pickles came back yesterday. That's
good, I guess, although I already have scratch
marks on my arms from her. I kind of missed
her, but now that she's back, I remember how

annoying she is when she wants attention. Anyway, watch out, RJ. She can be vicious with paper that is left lying around!

Yours truly,
Arthur Bean

▶▶ ▶▶ ▶▶

Peer Tutoring Program — Progress Report
Session: November 16th
Worked On: Homonyms

Ms W, I don't know what Arthur's problem is, but hes the worst tutor ever. Their must be another guy out there.
— Robbie

Ms Whitehead,

It's my belief that if Robbie actually paid attention to what I was saying, he may actually have learned what a homonym is, rather than using it for an hour as an insult about my "girly-man" nature.

— Arthur

Assignment: Shakespearean Reflections

We are starting our unit on *A Midsummer Night's Dream* this week. It's a great play, full of romance and adventure, and it's very funny too! To prepare, I would like you to write two short paragraphs, imagining yourself as an actor or an audience member in Shakespeare's time. What does it feel like to be onstage? What does it smell like? What are you wearing? Did you have to sneak in to see the show, or are you rich enough to buy a seat? Please use at least seven adjectives and five adverbs in describing the scene you create.

Due: November 18

▶▶ ▶▶ ▶▶

My Life as Shakespeare

By Arthur Bean

The Globe Theatre is putting on my play again tonight. It's wonderfully exciting that they created this whole theatre just for me. I adjust my funny looking wig and smooth out my greasy moustache. It smells in here, like it does every night. It's too bad that the audience doesn't bathe ever. The stench of onions and garlic swirls around me disgustingly. It also smells strongly of rancid feet. It reminds me of my own father's feet when he takes off his boots after spending the day doing farm work, but a hundred thousand times worse. I gag quietly, so that the actors don't hear me. I don't want them to think I don't like their acting.

The thing is, though, that I don't like their acting. The guy playing the king is OK, but the prince is really overbearing, saying all his lines too quickly and loudly. There is no emotion in his voice. But the audience doesn't mind. They clap loudly and call out adjectives like Wonderful!, Fantastic!, Grandly delightful!, Hilariously terrific! and "Stupendous work, Mr. Shakespeare!" Thankfully, they can see that I'm the really brilliant person in this round theatre tonight.

Arthur, this is some nice work in describing how Shakespeare might feel about his work. However, I was hoping that you would focus more on the atmosphere of the play, rather than on the opinions of the playwright. Also, I don't appreciate your subtle mocking of the assignment parameters. It's unpleasant and unnecessary. This is a learning environment, and learning the rules of grammar will make you a better writer. I suggest you take these things more seriously in future assignments.

Ms Whitehead

▶▶ ▶▶ ▶▶

From: Kennedy Laurel (imsocutekl@hotmail.com)
To: Arthur Bean (arthuraaronbean@gmail.com)
Sent: November 20, 10:00

Hi Arthur!

How's your story coming?? I LOVE that we get to write whatever we want! I told my mom that I had to watch a bunch of movies as RESEARCH for my story LOL!

I was thinking that maybe we could swap story beginnings soon! I have part of my story (like, the first part!), but I was hoping to get your feedback BEFORE I go too far LOL! I am having trouble with my main character! Right now it's a man, but I THINK it might be more fun to have it be a woman! GRRRL POWER LOL!!! I also changed my vampire idea into ALIENS. Vampires are so last year LOL!

Anyway, do you have a new idea? Let me know if you want to swap soon! I think that's how this is supposed to work with partners, right LOL?!

Kennedy ☺

From: Arthur Bean (arthuraaronbean@gmail.com)
To: Kennedy Laurel (imsocutekl@hotmail.com)
Sent: November 20, 10:20

Dear Kennedy,

I think that swapping stories is a great idea! Of course, mine is still very rough, so I'm not sure how much I'll have to share with you. I've really been focusing my energy on writing my novel. But I would love to read your story and give you my edits. Having not read it, I know I can't say this yet, but I think having a girl as a main character is a great idea. My mom read a lot of science fiction and always complained that the women in the books were only sex objects. So I say go for it!

Yours truly,
Arthur Bean

From: Kennedy Laurel (imsocutekl@hotmail.com)
To: Arthur Bean (arthuraaronbean@gmail.com)
Sent: November 20, 18:19

Awesome, Arthur!!! I'll change it and send you something next week, and you can do the same if you want!
    Maybe your mom can read my story too, since she's a sci-fi expert LOL!!!

K ☺

From: Arthur Bean (arthuraaronbean@gmail.com)
To: Kennedy Laurel (imsocutekl@hotmail.com)
Sent: November 20, 18:23

Hi, Kennedy,

My mom can't read your story. She's dead. Sorry about that. I guess you'll have to make do with just me.

Yours truly,
Arthur Bean

▶▶ ▶▶ ▶▶

From: Kennedy Laurel (imsocutekl@hotmail.com)
To: Arthur Bean (arthuraaronbean@gmail.com)
Sent: November 21, 9:04

Arthur! I am soooooo sorry! I felt awful when I
read your email last night!!! What a terrible friend,
bringing up your mom like that! I cried a LOT when
I read that. I had no idea! I'm so sorry if I made you
sad by bringing it up! That's so sad! I'm amazed
that you don't talk about it more at school and stuff!
Then I remembered that you started school late
and TOTALLY realized that must be why! I'm such a
JERK!
   If you ever want to talk about it, or even just need a
hug, I'm here!!

I'm sorry!
Kennedy ☹

From: Arthur Bean (arthuraaronbean@gmail.com)
To: Kennedy Laurel (imsocutekl@hotmail.com)
Sent: November 21, 10:35

Dear Kennedy,

I'm so sorry that I made you feel bad! I didn't mean
to! Sometimes I don't know how to say sad stuff.
   She died at the end of last school year. It was really
sad. She was the speech therapist at my school. She
came in once a week and worked with different kids
with lisps and who talked funny. One day she didn't
come in, because she had a brain aneurysm at home
and died right then. I was really mad at her because
I had to take the bus home that day, and I always

looked forward to not taking the bus on Thursdays. I remember getting ready to yell at her about it, especially because it was after I did really badly on a Math test. There were a couple of kids in my class who hated her because she made them do extra homework to practise speaking like everyone else. They called her Mrs. Mean. I guess she was pretty mean sometimes, but I didn't like that everyone knew that my mom was kind of mean sometimes. After she died, no one had to go to speech therapy class. I think most of the kids who went were pretty glad about that. I wasn't glad though.

I still sometimes get mad at her for stuff she used to do, but then I get mad about being mad. She was really nice too. My dad called her the Queen Bean, and she thought that was really funny and made beans for dinner every Sunday, no matter what. Since she died, my dad and I never eat beans anymore. Isn't that weird? I guess not that weird. We don't really have fancy dinners on Sundays anymore either.

Anyway, it totally sucked and I try not to think about it or talk about it because it still sucks. But I still think about her every day. My neighbour Nicole taught me to knit because she said that busy hands make a quiet mind. I don't think that's true, but maybe it works. If nothing else, I can make really good hats!

Anyway, I'm going to be a famous writer and dedicate my first book to my mom. I think she would have liked that. I mean, my novel is practically done anyway.

I don't know why I'm writing all this to you! I'm sorry! I just thought maybe you would feel better if you knew some of the story too. Maybe it's worse, I don't know. I've never had a mom who died before.

Actually, I don't know anyone else who has died. I guess that's a good thing. Anyway, I don't really know what to say about it.

I can't wait to read your story next week. I will work on having something really good too. And I'll take you up on that hug too!

Yours truly,
Arthur Bean

From: Kennedy Laurel (imsocutekl@hotmail.com)
To: Arthur Bean (arthuraaronbean@gmail.com)
Sent: November 21, 14:05

Hi Arthur!

I'm so glad that you did tell me! I had no idea! That's really sad — I wish for your sake that you had gotten to say good-bye to her! I kind of understand how you feel. My grandpa died last year, but he had cancer. That was hard too! I hated having to visit him in the hospital when he was so sick, but then I hated MYSELF for hating visiting my grandpa! It was AWFUL!

I think it's really impressive how well you are doing! You DEFINITELY still have your sense of humour, which is kind of AMAZING! I would probably want to drop out of school if anyone in my family died! Your email also makes me sad that sometimes I wish that something BAD would happen to my mom when she's yelling at me about doing my homework or cleaning my room! I don't really want that to happen, but SOMETIMES she is SO ANNOYING! I can't believe I am admitting this! I'm a TERRIBLE person!

Anyway, I just wanted to say that I think you are

AWESOME and you can send me emails WHENEVER you're sad if you want! And I think you should dedicate your first book to her — that would be so nice!

Kennedy ☺

▶▶ ▶▶ ▶▶

Peer Tutoring Program — Progress Report
Session: November 23rd
Worked On: Shakespeare's Time

Ms W, even tho his hair looked really dumb today, artie was kind of helpful in checking my Shakspear assinement for misstakes.
— Robbie

Robert spent a lot of time today either talking to his friends at other tables or insulting my new haircut and coming up with rude words that rhyme with Artie.
— Arthur

▶▶ ▶▶ ▶▶

November 24th

Dear RJ,

I've been reading a lot of terrible things recently, so I thought I would tell you about them.

The first one was Robbie's "Life in Shakespeare's Time" assignment. His writing is really, *really* bad, but his ideas are kind of interesting. He wrote this whole thing about being poor and not being able to get into the show, but listening to it while begging on the street. It was kind of sad, because his character couldn't have what he wanted, which was actually just to watch a play. But then he makes these stupid mistakes, like saying that the beggar would go to the food bank. Everyone knows that there was no food bank in the Middle Ages. Like I said, stupid. But I liked his idea. He seems to have all these stories ready all the time. I guess that's what makes him such a good liar. Maybe that's why I can't write any stories these days.

So that was the first terrible thing I had to read. The second thing was in the newspaper at school. Kennedy's boyfriend put in this like . . . ad-thing . . . saying that he thought she was cute and nice. Those were the words he used! Cute and nice! Those are words I use to describe Pickles. And Pickles is a nine-year-old cat. It's so lame! Then in Gym class, she was all giggly about it, and I saw the newspaper cut out and hanging up in her locker the other day. Although it was underneath her movie poster of *District Nine*, so at least it's not surrounded by hearts or anything.

Then I read Kennedy's email asking for my

mom to read her story. That made me pretty sad, and then I felt bad that I made her sad too. I just don't know what to say about it. It's not like there's a magical way to tell people. It hadn't come up in conversation. I'm not going to be running laps beside Kennedy and casually say, "Oh, hi, Kennedy! Did I ever mention that my mom is dead? How many laps is this for you? Oh, nine? Yeah, I'm on my fourth. Well, see you around . . . the track." Hahaha.

That little joke was for you, RJ. I know you like a good one-liner. Nicole says that joking about death makes people uncomfortable, but I don't know how else to talk about it. You know me, RJ. I'm a joker! I'm just glad that Kennedy didn't seem weirded out by my email. She's so awesome. I kind of love that she admitted that she's not perfect. It makes her even more perfect.

And the last terrible thing I read was the first act of *A Midsummer Night's Dream*.

Ms Whitehead is all "This is the greatest" and she laughs fakely at what Shakespeare called jokes. But I don't get it. It's all "thou" and "thee," and I know people think it's brilliant, but I think they just want to feel smart. I can't believe we have to study this all the way until Christmas holidays. How am I supposed to get any inspiration for my own award-winning story from crappy plays like this one?

Yours truly,
Arthur Bean

▸▸ ▸▸ ▸▸

From: Kennedy Laurel (imsocutekl@hotmail.com)
To: Arthur Bean (arthuraaronbean@gmail.com)
Sent: November 28, 21:21

Hi Arthur!!!

OK, below is the BEGINNING of my story for the competition! I changed to a girl main character like you suggested, and she is AWESOME! Let me know your opinions — be HONEST! I want to win LOL!!! Can't wait to read your beginning too! Send it to me whenever and I will read it post-haste LOL! (We're reading Shakespeare in English class, and they say things like post-haste LOL!)
   OK! Be honest (but I hope you like it!).

Kennedy ☺

Untitled Story! LOL

The brains of the alien were lavender and grey, and splattered all over Sophie's perfectly matched brown and pink off-the-shoulder top and skinny jeans. She flicked her high ponytail over her shoulder, showing off her tiny, pink rosebud earrings.

"Well? What should we do with it now?" she asked nonchalantly, slinging her bazooka over her left shoulder. She wiped the gory blood from her hands on her back pockets and looked over at her partner.

"I'd say we should bury it. Deep. Real deep," Tom replied in his sombre bass tones. He looked at his own navy coveralls, covered with a red and green flannel shirt.

"Well, I guess we should start digging," Sophie sighed, reaching for the shovel . . .

Sophie woke with a start. She'd had that dream again. She tried to sit up, but found that her arms were still in the restraints locked to the rails of her bed. She pulled hard, but the restraints just cut into her wrists again, leaving her writhing in pain. She yelled out, "Nurse!" But no one came. No one ever came during the daytime. Only if you screamed and cursed in the middle of the night would the nurses come, with their long needles glinting off the fluorescent lights of the hallway like golden teeth.

"You need to keep it down over there. They'll hear you," whispered the scratchy voice of the old woman in the bed next to Sophie. "They'll come, and they'll bite off your nose and your fingernails, and they won't stop." The old woman cackled madly. "Of course, I wouldn't mind if they ate my fingers . . . I've been trying to chew them off for years!" The woman's violet hospital gown was drooping, and her white hair was falling out. Or maybe she had pulled it out . . .

Sophie shivered. It had been fifteen days that she had been in the hospital, and the dreams were getting worse. Dreams, though? No. She knew they were more than that. The aliens were real. She had seen them. She had strangled one until its eyeballs burst out of its head in a gargantuan mess of crimson and white and light blue tendons, all over her favourite teal dress, the one with the black piping and oversized buttons at the collar. She couldn't make that up. And she had the dry cleaning bill to prove it.

From: Arthur Bean (arthuraaronbean@gmail.com)
To: Kennedy Laurel (imsocutekl@hotmail.com)
Sent: November 29, 8:07

Wow, Kennedy! This is amazing! I think you've done a great job on starting your story. It's really scary. I can't wait to see what happens next.

There's just one thing. I don't really get why you've described all of the outfits of the characters. And would they have a dry cleaner? That's weird. It seems out of place. I don't think you need those parts.

Yours truly,
Arthur Bean

November 29th

Dear RJ,

I read Kennedy's story beginning, and it's pretty great. I don't even know where to start. Mine needs to be better than Kennedy's story. I mean, I have lots of time, but I can't believe she's started already! Mine will be funny, sad, scary AND provocative. Sure, Sockland was great when I was in grade six, but now I'm in grade seven. I have to do something amazing, and I've got zip.

To get inspired, I borrowed a copy of *The Shining* by Stephen King from Nicole's bookshelf yesterday. I figured it was OK because I live right next door and I plan on returning it when I'm done, but I didn't tell her that I took it. Nicole is pretty laid back about stuff like that. Whenever she has friends over she's always like, "Take it!

Bring it back whenever!" And since the librarian at the public library won't let me take out adult books after that time my mom got angry at her for allowing me to take out the movie *The Exorcist*, and then I didn't sleep for two months, I kind of have to borrow it under the radar. I want to read it because Stephen King is really famous and has written over a hundred books, so it must be amazing.

I don't think *The Shining* can be that scary though. It's got a kid in it, and the family lives in a hotel, but it's like a haunted hotel. I wish we lived in a hotel instead of an apartment. That sounds pretty cool to me. It sounds like a Disney movie plot!

Yours truly,
Arthur Bean

DECEMBER

December 1st

To Whom It May Concern,
    Please excuse Arthur Bean's absence
from school the past two days. He has
been having trouble sleeping, and has
had migraines in the mornings. Should
you have any questions, please call me.

Many thanks,
Ernie B.

December 1st

Dear RJ,

The Shining is the scariest book ever written,
but I couldn't stop reading it! And I can't tell if
Stephen King is a genius or just a psycho. There
were crazy ghosts and axes and murders and
stuff. There was even a maze where the main guy
chases his wife and kid through the maze in the
dark and snow. I'm never going into a labyrinth
ever! It was so intense and I kept dreaming about
it. Who comes up with this stuff?

Yours truly,
Arthur Bean

▶▶ ▶▶ ▶▶

Peer Tutoring Program — Progress Report
Session: December 2nd
Worked On: Shakespeare Stuff

Ms W, when even Artie dosn't like Shakespear,
why do we all have to suffer? We talked today
about how the school board should be changing
the curricculum. how we should watch more
movies in class. Artie calls it "vissual litteracy".
its pretty important to us as the leaders of
tomorro, and we think you should look into
changing the curiculum for next year.
— Robbie

Ms Whitehead, it's possible that Robbie and I
have a shared hatred of overwritten plot lines
and fancy words used for no reason. I think that
says something.
— Arthur

From: Kennedy Laurel (imsocutekl@hotmail.com)
To: Arthur Bean (arthuraaronbean@gmail.com)
Sent: December 2, 17:32

Hi Arthur!

Thanks for your suggestions! I KNOW there wouldn't
be dry cleaning, silly! It was a JOKE, but I guess
not a very good one LOL! I can't WAIT to read your

beginning! Do you want to send it to me?! I have LOTS of time this week since our Math teacher has the flu! No more circle graphs LOL!

Kennedy ☺

From: Arthur Bean (arthuraaronbean@gmail.com)
To: Kennedy Laurel (imsocutekl@hotmail.com)
Sent: December 2, 19:56

Dear Kennedy,

I don't have anything to send to you yet. I find my best method of work is to fully visualize my piece, and then I like to write it on paper first. I find the sound of the pencil on paper is very creatively stimulating. But I can tell you what my story will be about. It's about a man and his family who live in a hotel. He's a writer, but the ghosts in the hotel also haunt him. Then he goes crazy and tries to kill his family with an axe. His son is also psychic, and can call up other psychic people, but his son also plays with the ghosts and goes a little crazy. And the man's wife doesn't know what to do, so she cries all the time. She will run around in a maze in a blizzard too, and she might die. It will likely be very frightening.

Yours truly,
Arthur Bean

From: Kennedy Laurel (imsocutekl@hotmail.com)
To: Arthur Bean (arthuraaronbean@gmail.com)
Sent: December 2, 20:18

Wow Arthur!! That sounds . . . um . . . complicated.
But great!!! Scary though, that the man goes after
his family with an axe! It sounds like one of those
horror books my dad reads by Steven King or like a
V.C. Andrews book (I LOVE her books!!) or something!
I hope they all make it out of the hotel ok!

Are you writing something for the last edition of
the *Marathon* this year? I'm doing an interview with
Sandy on winning the boys' volleyball championship!
I already told him that I wasn't going to go easy on
him just because I'm his GIRLFRIEND! I'll be like Lois
Lane interviewing Superman LOL! I can't BELIEVE it's
already so close to Christmas LOL!! Any suggestions
of what guys like? I have to get something for my
boyfriend LOL!

From: Arthur Bean (arthuraaronbean@gmail.com)
To: Kennedy Laurel (imsocutekl@hotmail.com)
Sent: December 2, 21:09

Dear Kennedy,

I guess that plot does sound a little complicated for a
short story. Maybe I will look at doing something else.
Back to the drawing board . . .

Yours truly,
Arthur Bean

▶▶ ▶▶ ▶▶

A Day in the Life: An Oscar-worthy Film

By Arthur Bean

The AV Club at Terry Fox Jr. High is showing their first feature this week in the Drama room. *A Day in the Life* is a poignant and gripping account of an ordinary day at Terry Fox Jr. High School. Shot as though seen through the eyes of an unnamed narrator, *A Day in the Life* follows an "ordinary" student through a day at school. Though the day begins normally, the heavy silence in the film clearly foreshadows the disaster that befalls at the end of the movie — a test in Science. Horrors! Our beloved narrator is clearly unprepared for such a crisis!

A Day in the Life is reminiscent of the early work of Francis Ford Coppola, a surprise considering its collaborative directorial nature. A different AV Club member has directed each scene, but this pastiche of styles makes it even more interesting. For example, each director uses music to its fullest emotional range, including the unique work of grade eight student Liam Hasser, who uses Van Halen's *Jump!* as the soundtrack for the basketball unit in Gym. The supporting cast is equally as strong as the low voice of the narrator (played impeccably by grade nine student Alfonso Millar). He sounded almost like Darth Vader. It was very sinister! Of particular note is the performance of Mr. Everett in an understated but nuanced walk-on role as The Teacher.

Some viewers with weaker stomachs may find the classroom scenes too much to handle. The emotion in the film can be overwhelming, so bring your handkerchief for a heart-wrenching scene that takes place during Math class. This is a scene that will clearly be discussed in film critic circles for years to come.

A Day in the Life plays in the Drama room from 12:00–1:00 all week December 6–10. See it before someone spoils the twist ending!

Hiya, Arthur,

You definitely covered all the elements of the film! However, I am having trouble understanding the tone of your piece — are you being sincere, or sarcastic? Maybe you thought that my performance wouldn't win me any Golden Globes? The shock of it! Good-bye, Hollywood! Your praise is overwhelming, and some readers may read it as being insincere. If you're available, we can meet during a lunch hour to discuss changes to your review. It would be great to see you take some of the feedback from earlier articles and apply it to your next piece, OK, buddy?

Mr. E.

Dear Mr. Everett,

You told me to be more positive in my articles. This is as positive as I can be, particularly for one of the most boring movies I have ever sat through. And my dad made me watch Citizen Kane once, so I know what boring movies look like.

Perhaps my own series of articles would be a better way for me to use my editorial skills. I'd love to meet with you to talk about my ideas for articles!

Yours truly,
Arthur Bean

▸▸ ▸▸ ▸▸

JUNIOR AUTHORS CONTEST

Just a reminder to work on your stories during the
winter break! Final drafts of your stories are due
April 1st, no exceptions! Finalists in the school will
be published in the spring edition of the *Marathon*,
and put to a school-wide vote.
Remember to use your creative writing partners for advice,
editing and as a sounding board for your great ideas! Should
you have any questions before the holidays, please see Ms
Whitehead by 4 p.m. on December 17th. Happy writing!

▶▶ ▶▶ ▶▶

Assignment: Character Diaries

Choose your favourite character from *A Midsummer Night's Dream*
and write a diary entry referencing a scene from the play. Your
diary entry should demonstrate your understanding of the material
we have covered and show some insight into how the character
may be feeling at a certain moment in the play.

Due: December 9

▶▶ ▶▶ ▶▶

Peer Tutoring Program — Progress Report
Session: December 7th
Worked On: Shakespeare Diary Assignment

We edited Robbie's assignment. It went alright.
— Arthur

here is my assinement that Artie helped me
with. He also moved around some sentences and
made it sound more nice. We also worked on
some better rhimes for my love pome. Here it is.
— Robbie

dear diary,

I am in love with Hermia, but she is in love
with Lysander. This is terrible. I try so hard to
make her like me, but nothing works. I've known
her forever. We've played sports together since
we were in Italian kindergarten. But she just
thinks of me as a friend, and wants me to be in
love with her friend Helena. Helena is ugly, and
told me that I was stupid and the worst shortstop
she had ever seen. But Hermia is still really nice
to me. I just wish she wasn't running away with
Lysander, because I get really bad hay fever in the
forest, and it's even worse at night.

When I catch up with her and Lysander, I am
going to give her this love poem that I wrote.

Hermia Hermia. You are a beaut
I think you are nice. I think you are cute.
I like your sweet smile. I like your round face.
So go out with me now, and show your good taste.

Later Diary,
Demetrius

▶▶ ▶▶ ▶▶

December 8th

Dear RJ,

Today would have been my mom's birthday. I
stayed home from school and Dad stayed home
from work. It was weird. Neither of us really
wanted to do anything. I just wanted to stay in
bed and read a book or something, and I think
Dad probably wanted to just sit in his room too.
But then that felt weird too, so we went and got
flowers and went to the cemetery.

I don't know what to say to my dad when he
is so quiet, so I didn't say anything. He didn't
say anything either. Neither of us said anything,
we just put the roses down and stood there.

It was freezing outside. I really just wanted
to leave because I had forgotten my mittens. It
started to snow too, and normally I like snow
because it makes the city quiet, but today it
made the cemetery even quieter and weirder.
The worst part was when I thought about how
Mom was always talking a lot, and how it would
have been better if she was there to make it less
awkward.

Yours truly,
Arthur Bean

▶▶ ▶▶ ▶▶

Demetrius's Diary

By Arthur Bean

Dear Diary,

> Oh, Hermia, your smile is so great
> And your teeth are so white and so straight.
> You come from a country shaped like a boot
> And your laugh is so pretty and your face is so cute.
> Will you be my girlfriend and then maybe my wife?
> For I know I will love you the rest of my life.

This is the love poem I would like to give
Hermia. Alas, I cannot, for she is in love with
Lysander. I think it's sad that she's in love with
him, when I have clearly loved her since I met
her in Italian Gym class so long ago. Hermia
thinks I should be in love with Helena, but
Helena looks like a horse, with giant teeth and
a long nose. I love Hermia.

I will have to follow her and Lysander into the
forest tonight and give her my love poem.

Arthur,

Your assignment is remarkably similar
to Robbie's work, using an identical
style, the same themes and identical
characters. Please see me after class
to explain these similarities, keeping in
mind that plagiarism can be of both
published and unpublished works. I take
this very seriously, and expect that
you will too. I hope that your burst of
creativity in this assignment is merely

*an unfortunate coincidence, and not
because you helped Robbie with his
assignment this week.*

Ms Whitehead

▶▶ ▶▶ ▶▶

December 10th

Dear RJ,

I can't win. Ms Whitehead hates me. She's
made it pretty clear. I think she must have been
secretly heartbroken by a famous author when
she was young. I bet she met him in college and
he told her she was pretty, and then broke up
with her because she told him that his work was
lazy. But he was just being deep without using
a lot of words. Lots of famous writers let things
stay below the surface. Or maybe he thought
that the assignment was stupid and not worth
his time. That happens. Then she probably
got all mad at him about it, and he realized
that she would always be telling him that his
writing sucked and that he was being lazy. So
he dumped her. And now she's taking it out on
me. I bet I remind her of him because I wear
cool hats and show promise as a famous writer.
She's jealous of my talent. I bet she never wrote
anything good ever. She'll never choose my story
for the school competition, even if it is the best
one, I know it. Well, I'll show her. My story is
going to be way better than all of them. It will be
better than her stupid "brilliant" Shakespeare,

because no one understands that, and no one cares about the stupid diary entries of an old play.

Yours truly,
Arthur Bean

▶▶ ▶▶ ▶▶

Assignment: Holiday Free-Form Writing

Happy holidays! In this assignment I want you to indulge your creative spirit! There are no boundaries, no structure and no rules here; just write something you want to write. It can be a poem, a short story, a diary entry of a fictional character, a memoir from your childhood — anything that inspires you to write! Let your inner artist soar on the paper!

Due: December 15

December 15th

Dear RJ,

Here's a thing I wrote for Ms Whitehead's class, but then I decided not to hand it in. I don't think it's very good, so I'm going to hand in something different. But I wanted to put this somewhere, and you seem like the kind of guy who would appreciate it. Let me know what you think. . . . Hahaha!

Yours truly,
Arthur Bean

A Christmas Story

My dad bought a Christmas tree this past
weekend. He went to the lot and picked it out
while I stayed home and watched whatever
movie was on the TV on Sunday afternoon.
When he came home, he left it sitting on top
of the car until dinner, when I saw it and
said, "Hey, Dad. There's a tree on the car." He
mumbled something about it being an impulse
buy. He even bought a stand even though I
know we already have one somewhere. I guess
now we have two. But I didn't say anything. I
just helped him pull it off the car, and we set it
up in the living room, right beside the television.

There were old sitcom reruns playing on
the television the whole time. I made us Kraft
Dinner, and my dad had a beer and watched
TV. He never picked up the remote control to
change the channel, he just sat there watching
the television on the same channel I had been
watching, and I listened to the sounds of canned
laughter as I stirred in the cheese. As the tree
warmed up, it dropped its branches and began
to lean to the left, and soon half of the tree
was blocking the television. I noticed it during
dinner, but I didn't say anything. I don't think
my dad noticed. We just sat there with our
empty plates covered in drying cheese sauce
on the floor beside the couch.

After a couple of days, I asked my dad
if we were going to decorate it, but he said
that he didn't know where Mom had kept the
decorations. So the tree sits in the living room,
blocking the television. Its needles are falling off,

and we haven't watered it in days. It is empty
of lights and balls and glittery tin soldiers and
nutcrackers, but still full of the memories of
Christmases past.

Yours truly,
Arthur Bean

Assignment: A Christmas Story

By Arthur Bean

The best day of last Christmas was the day
when my dad brought home the Christmas
tree. My mom had gotten out all the Christmas
ornaments and sang along loudly to "The Twelve
Days of Christmas" while she untangled the
lights.

My dad showed up at home with the biggest
tree I had ever seen, and together we dragged our
tree off the roof of the car and into the house.
The pine smell filled the room, and then my
dad swore and swore while he tried to get the
lights on straight. My mother would yell at him
every time a bad word came out of his mouth,
and I would laugh at them while I unwrapped
the ornaments and lined them up on the coffee
table. We got all the ornaments on the tree, and
my dad drank a beer, and my mom had a wine
cooler, and I had hot chocolate and we sat on the
couch and stared at the Christmas tree until the
sun went down and the only light in the house
came from the bright red and blue lights that
twisted and turned around the tree.

That night, very late, there was a tinkling

sound. The bells on the tree were singing wildly, and I woke up and listened to them in my bed. Then they got louder, and louder, until I heard a *CRRRRACK*, and then a crashing noise, full of breaking glass.

We ran out into the living room, and Pickles was cowering in the corner behind the couch, where she had gotten stuck after batting at the lowest ornaments on the tree until the tree fell over. My dad swore a lot, and my mom laughed and laughed, and she picked up the cat in one hand and went and got the broom. She swept up all the glass and I held the dustpan while my dad propped up the tree again. We had to turn the tree around so that the back was facing the front, since it was too late to buy new Christmas lights and the branches were all broken. But I still think it was the nicest Christmas tree we ever had.

Dear Arthur,

Thank you for sharing a lovely Christmas memory of your mother with me. I hope you and your father have a nice holiday. See you in the New Year!

Ms Whitehead

▶▶ ▶▶ ▶▶

December 20th

Dear RJ,

Dad and I went Christmas shopping today
at the mall and we ran into Ms Whitehead!
It was SO awkward. We were eating lunch in
the food court, and she came around with her
taco combo looking for a seat. She didn't even
notice me at first. She just saw a free seat at
our table and asked if she could sit down. Then
she actually saw me and was all excited that
she got to meet my dad "since he had missed
the parent-teacher conference" (I think she was
judging him a little bit when she said that), and
freaked out about what a coincidence it was
that she ran into us. It was so over the top. I
wonder if she planned it. Maybe she was hitting
on my dad, since she knows that he's single
now. That would not be cool.

   Anyway, she sat down with us and was
talking all about her Christmas plans. She
even asked my dad for his advice on a plaid
shirt she bought for her brother. Like he knows
anything about fashion! She had all kinds of
bags too, including one from the lingerie store.
I was embarrassed for her. I can't believe she
was buying underwear and then sitting with
a student! Who does that?? She said that she
was going home to Toronto for Christmas,
and that she was taking her grandmother to
see *The Nutcracker*. She said she goes with
her grandmother every year. I don't know how
she still has a grandmother who is still alive! I

wonder how old she is? I thought she was forty.

When we left, she gave me a hug and shook my dad's hand. It was a total surprise, so I hugged her back. I hope no one from school saw me hugging my teacher. That's how rumours get started.

Yours truly,
Arthur

▶▶ ▶▶ ▶▶

From: Kennedy Laurel (imsocutekl@hotmail.com)
To: Arthur Bean (arthuraaronbean@gmail.com)
Sent: December 21, 17:56

Hi Arthur ☹

How's your Christmas break??? Mine is TERRIBLE. ☹
Sandy broke up with me!!! ☹☹ He said that he was too busy to have a girlfriend right now!! I guess that he is really busy with friends and stuff. And I want to understand because I love him a lot. I cried a lot when he told me, but I told him that I want to still be friends. I think that we will be friends, especially since I know he's just going through a hard time right now, and he'll want to get back together after Christmas break when we are at school again I think! He's even failing HEALTH class. Everyone knows that's a joke class! But he's really smart, so I think he's just being pulled in too many directions. But Arthur!!!! I love Sandy SO much!!!! I already miss him!! Normally we would talk on the phone or text all night!!! I already bought him a Christmas present too!! Can I still give it to him? It will show that I care

about him still, right??? You're a guy, so you would know better than my girlfriends!!

ANYWAYS, I feel so sad ☹☹☹ WORST CHRISTMAS EVER!!! ☹

Kennedy ☹

From: Arthur Bean (arthuraaronbean@gmail.com)
To: Kennedy Laurel (imsocutekl@hotmail.com)
Sent: December 21, 18:19

Dear Kennedy,

I'm sorry to hear about your breakup. Boys that age can be very difficult to understand sometimes. I really feel badly for you! When you feel bad, I feel bad, so today is the worst day ever!

You should get some good ice cream. I think you're supposed to eat ice cream after a breakup, aren't you? And then I think you watch sappy movies or something. I'm sorry. I don't really know what to tell you. Just remember that you are the greatest girl ever, and you are super nice and smart and cute. Any guy in the school would love to be your boyfriend! Sandy was a total jerk anyway. If I were you, I wouldn't give him the present. Return it and get something cool for yourself. He doesn't deserve you!

I don't know if I can help at all, but if you want to hang out this Christmas break, maybe we can go see a movie or something. My cousins are coming in to stay with us for a while, but I would leave them behind if you need to talk. ☺

Yours truly,
Arthur Bean

December 21st

Dear RJ,

BEST DAY EVER!!!!

I think that Kennedy will realize soon that her old boyfriend was a super jerk, and we'll go out on a date. And we'll go see a scary movie and she'll squeal and hide her face in my shoulder and I'll hold her hand and laugh in that "I'm not laughing at you" way, and we'll hold hands all the way through the movie and down the escalator in the mall, and to the bus stop.

I bet she smells like fruity shampoo. I wonder if it's too late to ask for cologne for Christmas. I'll probably need it soon.

And my cousins are coming for Christmas break! I wish Luke lived closer. He's really popular and he has great stories about stuff he does. He comes up with great things to do too. Like, during the summer when we were at my grandparents' and all the adults were always around, he found this movie theatre playing weird matinees during the week. So we got dressed up in costumes and went to this terrible, really old alien movie. We threw popcorn at the screen and yelled at the characters and no one there minded! It was hilarious! Anyway, it'll be so great when Luke is here. I've already set up a sleeping bag on the floor of my room for him, and given him the best pillow from my bed. One more day!

Yours happily,
Arthur Bean!!

▸▸ ▸▸ ▸▸

December 27th

Dear RJ,

Merry Christmas, I guess. I don't have a lot
of time to write to you. We spent most of
Christmas Day at my grandparents' house, and
we just got back home to the apartment tonight.
Now the apartment is overfull, especially with
Luke and George and their parents staying
here. My dad is sleeping on the couch and gave
up his bed, and George has a sleeping bag
under the dining-room table. He seems to like
it there, especially since he never says anything
to anyone. Luke said that he's like that all the
time. It makes me glad that I don't have an older
brother like that.

Anyway, RJ, Christmas has been really
weird. No one leaves me by myself. My aunt
and my grandma keep hugging me and
getting teary and I just want them to leave
me alone. It's so different, because everyone
is pretending to be happy when we are all
together, so it's extra loud in the house and
the music is always playing. No one is even
mentioning the fact that my mom is gone or
that we used to go to church because my mom
wanted us to go or that my mom's stuffing was
way better. Every year I used to argue with my
mom about getting to open presents before we
ate breakfast on Christmas Day, and I always
lost, but that was OK because we always did
it. That argument was a tradition too. But
this year, I said, "Let's open presents before
breakfast," and everyone agreed. It's like no

one will say "No" to me no matter what. I told Luke this, and he dared me to ask Grandpa for a cigarette to prove my theory. I didn't, of course.

Anyway, I got some books and clothes and games and stuff, and Nicole got me a Stephen King book all about writing that should help me write my story. And now I can hear my aunt calling for me, because she thinks that I'm in here crying because I "shouldn't be alone in this difficult time." At least Luke is here. He's standing at the door making fun of me for doing homework over the break. If he only knew, RJ!!

Yours truly,
Arthur Bean

▶▶ ▶▶ ▶▶

From: Robbie Zack (robbiethegreat2000@hotmail.com)
To: Arthur Bean (arthuraaronbean@gmail.com)
Sent: December 28, 23:41

dude I herd that u stol my english assinement about Demetrius and hermia. Ur a DEADMAN when we get back to school.

▶▶ ▶▶ ▶▶

From: Arthur Bean(arthuraaronbean@gmail.com)
To: Robbie Zack (robbiethegreat2000@hotmail.com)
Sent: December 29, 10:03

Dear Mr. Zack,

I believe you may have the wrong email address for the person you are trying to reach. I am a very rich and powerful businessman who lives in New Mexico. I think you might be looking for a different Arthur Aaron Bean, one who lives in Canada and is a kid in a school there. However, I am sure that when you find the Arthur Bean you are looking for, you will realize that he is not the type of guy who would steal a Shakespeare English assignment. He must be a good guy. I would like to meet him one day and offer him a job making millions of dollars. I assume that he was going to write something similar to your idea anyway, but probably better, since your spelling is terrible.

Good luck finding the right Arthur Bean. I am off to a business meeting with the richest and most powerful men in America.

Yours truly,
Arthur Bean

From: Robbie Zack (robbiethegreat2000@hotmail.com)
To: Arthur Bean (arthuraaronbean@gmail.com)
Sent: December 30, 12:32

Ur so funny I forgot to laff. Maybe I will laff at u when I stick ur head in the toilet.

From: Arthur Bean (arthuraaronbean@gmail.com)
To: Robbie Zack (robbiethegreat2000@hotmail.com)
Sent: December 30, 14:30

Dear Robbie,

I didn't steal your story. As you may have noticed, I am in the same English class as you. We read the same books. At least, *I* read the books. Anyway, I helped you with your assignment, and I was already writing something too. Really, I think you stole my assignment. After all, who fixed the rhymes in your letter? I did. You said so yourself. So my assignment might be kind of like yours, but I'm pretty sure that I'm a better writer than you and have great ideas all by myself.

As a side note, how did you find out that I stole your story? That's weird. I could have explained to you what happened if your parents didn't take you out of school a week early to go to Hawaii. If you are going to stick anyone's head in a toilet, I suggest choosing your least favourite parent.

Yours truly,
Arthur Bean

▶▶ ▶▶ ▶▶

From: Kennedy Laurel (imsocutekl@hotmail.com)
To: Arthur Bean (arthuraaronbean@gmail.com)
Sent: December 31, 11:55

Happy New Year Arthur!

Sorry that I haven't been in touch! My family went skiing for Christmas! It was good, except my older brother is in university and thinks he's cool, so at the last minute he decided to stay at home by himself. I was so mad, and he totally got into this yelling match with my dad. Then my mom cried about it every day we were away. I don't know why he had to be so inconsiderate. It was CHRISTMAS. My dad and him are STILL not talking even though we're back now. It's so tense here! I ALMOST look forward to school again LOL!

Anyway, the skiing was good, and it was cool to be out of the city, and then I didn't have to think about my boyfriend. ☹ Sandy and I had a long talk just before Christmas, and I don't want to THINK about him OR talk about him anymore! I gave him his Christmas present and he was SO weird about it!!! I don't know what HIS problem is, but I'm moving on. At least, for now.

I've been trying to work on putting some of my sadness into my story for the contest! Speaking of the contest, did you get LOTS of writing done over the break?? I can't believe we go back to school in THREE days!! I feel like we were just there LOL!! Are you changing options in the winter?? I am switching from Band to Drama! I'm just not cut out to be a flute player!! Maybe I would do better as a tuba player LOL!!! But I LOVED the Shakespeare unit we did in English class, and I think the Drama Club is doing a Shakespeare play!

ANYWAY, if you want to send me your story, I would love to read the beginning! I still haven't seen anything you've written! Are you avoiding sending it to me LOL?!

What are you doing tonight for the New Year? I'm going to a party that my friend Kayla is having! Hopefully there are cute boys there LOL!!!

Kennedy ☺

From: Arthur Bean (arthuraaronbean@gmail.com)
To: Kennedy Laurel (imsocutekl@hotmail.com)
Sent: December 31, 14:13

Happy New Year to you too, Kennedy! Skiing sounds fun! I have never been skiing. I think I am more of a snowboard kind of guy.

Tonight I am hanging out with my cousins. My cousin Luke and his brother George are visiting us. It's pretty awesome. My cousin George is in grade ten so I think we'll go with him to a high school party. That's probably what we'll do, but I don't know for sure. I bet my dad will let him use the car to get us there too.

I think I'm also going to switch to Drama this semester, so we'll be in the same class! It's too bad that we only get to change our options. I would like very much to get rid of Science and Math ☺ I'm very excited for Drama class. Maybe we can be partners!

I have been writing also, but so far it's pretty vague. I like to start my writing at the end with the climax, and then work backwards. I find that it gives my stories a clear plot direction. So if I send it to you now, it will ruin the end! Or I would have to kill you for knowing the end . . . hahaha . . .

See you in a few days! Or, as Shakespeare would say, "See thou anon." ☺

Yours truly,
Arthur Bean

JANUARY

January 1st

Dear RJ,

It's probably best to write down my resolutions
for this year now so that I don't break any of
them before noon HAHAHA. Anyway, here are
my resolutions:

1. I will win the writing competition. This is
number one!!!
2. I will not leave my dishes in the sink for
longer than three days.
3. I will tell Kennedy I love her, and make her
love me back.
4. I will like Shakespeare's plays, and not just
pretend to like them.
5. I will knit a sweater for my dad.
6. I will read the newspaper more often to know
what is going on in the world.
7. I will read *War and Peace*.
8. I will try not to get annoyed with Robbie
Zack during tutoring sessions so that I don't
"accidentally" punch him in the head.
9. I will stop eating spicy food at school, since it
gives me really bad hiccups and then kids make
fun of me.

I think this is enough to strive for this year. I don't want to set my expectations too high.

Happy New Year, RJ!

Yours truly,
Arthur Bean

From: Kennedy Laurel (imsocutekl@hotmail.com)
To: Arthur Bean (arthuraaronbean@gmail.com)
Sent: January 1, 13:00

Hi Arthur!!!

How was your NYE party?? Mine was pretty fun! There was a karaoke machine LOL!!! I can't believe your cousin's name is George! That's so funny! I thought only old people were called George LOL!

After I sent you that email, I remembered that it was your first Christmas without your mom! I'm SO sorry! I should have remembered that and not talked about MY Christmas! I'm glad your cousins were there! I hope it wasn't TOO sad! I'm sending you a HUGE email hug!

I'm so excited that you will be in Drama with me! Robbie is going to be in the class too!! It took some convincing at the party last night, but he finally admitted that he loves Shakespeare too, so the three of us can be the witches in Macbeth LOL!!! Double double toil and trouble LOL!!!

Your last email was HILARIOUS! I'm glad that you haven't lost your sense of humour even though your Christmas must have been SO sad!!

Anyway, I don't want you to KILL me for knowing how your story ends before it begins LOL!!! Can't wait to see you in THE THEATRE LOL!!!

Kennedy ☺

From: Arthur Bean (arthuraaronbean@gmail.com)
To: Kennedy Laurel (imsocutekl@hotmail.com)
Sent: January 1, 13:05

Hi, Kennedy,

I didn't end up going to the party. George got food poisoning or something, so Luke and I watched movies until 3 a.m. It was fun anyway. They are leaving today, which is too bad because if they lived here you could meet my cousin Luke. Anyway, glad you had a nice NYE party. See you in a few days. Thanks for the email hug too. Christmas was fine, and it wasn't too sad. Luke got a new video game so we played that and it was awesome. Well, it was awesome once we returned it and got the game that worked with his PlayStation instead of the Nintendo version.

Yours truly,
Arthur Bean

▶▶ ▶▶ ▶▶

January 2nd

Dear RJ,

All right, RJ. It's time to get serious. No more
thinking about other stuff. I have a story
competition to win. It's going to be hard,
especially since Kennedy is about to fall in
love with me. I wonder how famous couples
deal with it when one person is more famous
than the other. Luckily, most girls at school
are always reading magazines that give them
love advice and information on famous people,
so I'm going to let Kennedy do the research on
that. Ha!

But no more jokes about love advice, RJ.
I'm going to just think about writing and work
on being famous, and then I can stop thinking
about my mom and worrying about my dad
(all his unwrapped presents are still sitting
under the tree — he hasn't even put them
away! Pickles has clawed through one of the
scarves I made for Dad already. I put the other
one away for him). From here, it's all about
me, RJ!

Yours truly,
Arthur Bean

▶▶ ▶▶ ▶▶

Assignment: Character Sketch

Our next unit is Creative Writing, and it's my favourite unit to teach! I hope that our assignments over the next few weeks inspire you to find new ways to tell stories. For those of you participating in the short story contest, you might find some of these exercises strengthen your story. For others, I hope that this unit inspires you to continue writing outside of the classroom.

Write a few short paragraphs about a person who means a lot to you. This assignment will be a jumping-off point for developing a character for a short story you will be writing later in this unit. What does this person wear? What do they eat for breakfast? How do they interact with other people? Focus on creating a full character sketch, looking at their positive and negative characteristics, as well as their physical traits and personality.

Due: January 7

▶▶ ▶▶ ▶▶

Peer Tutoring Program — Progress Report
Session: January 4th
Worked On: Character Sketches

Ms W: I dont feel right about shareing my work with Arthur Bean. He may steel it and use it for his own work
— Robbie

Robbie is overreacting to something he knows nothing about. Perhaps his parents shouldn't have taken him out of school early to go to Hawaii for Christmas. I believe all the sun has gone to his head. I tried to explain to him (the same way I explained to you) that my work might seem similar on first glance, but that it is much deeper when you look at it. The symbolism is clear to very smart people. However, my explanation fell on deaf ears, and Robbie just spent the hour spitting on my paper. This is a waste of time.
— Arthur Bean

▶▶ ▶▶ ▶▶

A Character Sketch of Margaret Bean

By Arthur Bean

Her name was Margaret Mary Bean, but she always went by Marg. She hated being called Margaret. Marg Bean loved the ocean. She grew up on the Prairies, but she always wanted to live beside the ocean. She always wore blue and green, and she read lots of books with blue covers or pictures of boats on the covers. She said that she found it soothing to have a blue-covered book, even if it was actually a book about pirates or something.

Marg's pants were always too short because her legs were really long. She tried to wear really big shirts to make it seem like her pants were long enough, but it actually just made her pants look even shorter.

Marg Bean was prettiest when she was watching television or reading a book. This was because her face would relax, and her mouth would be closed and her hands would stop moving. Any other time her face was always really tight, like she was sewing her eyebrows together in her mind. Marg Bean got tired walking almost anywhere, and then she would breathe through her mouth. It made her seem really old, and she kind of looked like she was embarrassed because her face would be beet red.

Her voice was always louder than someone would expect it to be, and she seemed to be yelling all the time, but she was actually just talking. She was the person in the public library that everyone looked at when she would ask for books at the counter. "DO YOU HAVE ISAAC ASIMOV BOOKS?" she would say, and the librarian would say in a voice even softer than the one he used with everyone else, "Why yes, they are just over in the corner over there." "ARTHUR, I WILL BE IN THE CORNER. LET ME KNOW WHEN YOU HAVE YOUR BOOKS." And everyone would then look to see who she was talking to, and they would raise their eyebrows and judge me, like they didn't like anyone who knew her.

Marg Bean always had porridge and coffee for breakfast. Her favourite lunch was egg salad sandwiches, as long as there were no green onions in the egg salad. Curry made her go to the bathroom a lot, and she thought pepper was too spicy. She made perfect roast beef, and always made asparagus to go with it, which is the best vegetable to eat with roast beef. She also made really good spaghetti and meatballs, but she said they were too much work to make all the time, so she only made them a couple of times.

If Marg Bean were a character in my book, she would be a zombie mom who was the leader of the zombie pack. She has to be a zombie, because she isn't alive, and vampires are stupid. She would be super strong and have a zombie cat companion who would kill zombie mice. This is because Marg Bean loved cats — even Pickles, who is actually part cat, part demon. She hated mice, but not as much as she hated spiders.

Dear Arthur,

Your character sketch is an excellent beginning to our short story unit. You have captured the essence of your mother's personality through your choice of moments in this character sketch. However, you don't need to make your mother a zombie in your book if you don't want to. Many great stories are reflections of the person in their prime and don't need to be completely true to life.

Ms Whitehead

▶▶ ▶▶ ▶▶

January 8th

Dear RJ,

Drama class started this week, and Kennedy is in it too! It's nice to be in a class with her where we don't have to sit at desks, and we can sit wherever we want. I will always sit

83

beside Kennedy and show her how charming
I am in real life every day. It might even be
OK that Robbie is in the class too, except that
he's always talking to Kennedy. They have this
thing from when they played baseball together.
It's this weird high-five thing they do all the
time and it's really dumb. We also have to sing
in class, which I think is stupid because it's
a Drama class, not a choir, but Mr. Tan said
that a good actor is a "triple threat" if he can
act, sing and dance. I would like to triple threat
Robbie out of the class, but not with acting,
singing and dancing. More like kick-boxing,
karate and ninja moves.

I've been writing too. I started a dumb
story in Ms Whitehead's class about zombie
cats, but it's definitely not going to be famous.
I tried to base it on Pickles, but she's not a
zombie, she's just kind of possessed. My story
for the contest will make readers laugh and
cry and realize how smart I am. I'm going to
write something really deep. I think it needs to
have lots of description. Ms Whitehead is big
on description.

*The computer sat alone on the table, in
a faded grey room. The chair was brown,
cracked leather digging into anyone who sat
on it. The sun shone yellow through the dirty
windowpanes. There was nothing more to
say . . .*

Yours truly,
Arthur Bean

▶▶ ▶▶ ▶▶

Assignment: Interview a Friend

As we heard in our author talk today, some authors sit down and think about interviewing their characters to help develop back stories and other quirks that can turn a flat character into a well-rounded one. To practise this technique, I would like you to interview someone in your life. Come up with five questions that you feel will provide you with an accurate portrait of this person's likes and dislikes, and provide some insight into their outlook on life. In your assignment, please provide both the questions you posed and the answers from your interviewee.

Due: January 14

▶▶ ▶▶ ▶▶

**Peer Tutoring Program — Progress Report
Session: January 11th
Worked On: Interviews**

Artie was really rude today, and I even tried to be nice to the looser. He refused to help me fix my interveiw with Kennedy to make it a better assignment. I dont know how you think this tutoring is good for ether of us can we change now? Hes in my drama class now to and hes as annoying there as every where else.
— Robbie

Ms Whitehead: I would like an extension on this assignment. I was going to interview Kennedy Laurel, but Robbie already interviewed her. My interview was going to be much more in-depth, but I don't want you to think that I stole his idea. If anything, I think he stole mine, because I was talking to Kennedy in Drama class and it was pretty clear that I was going to ask her to be my person to interview. Now I have to think of a new person

to interview, and I don't know if I will have
time to do that by Friday.
— Arthur

*Arthur, I will give you time to interview
Robbie during class on Thursday, which
should give you enough time to hand in
your interview for Monday morning.*

Ms Whitehead

From: Kennedy Laurel (imsocutekl@hotmail.com)
To: Arthur Bean (arthuraaronbean@gmail.com)
Sent: January 15, 15:20

Hi Arthur! How much fun is Drama class!?! Mr. Tan
was saying that there are going to be auditions for
Romeo and Juliet soon! How awesome will that be?!
I'll answer that for you: SO AWESOME LOL!!!

ANYWAY, how is your story coming along? I totally
realized that I haven't read ANY of it yet! I think
I'm almost done mine! I made it so that the aliens
are really good at mind control and then my main
character doesn't know if she's under MIND CONTROL
or if it's all a dream! If you want, you can send me
your outline!! Of course, only if you've actually written
something! Just kidding — I'm just making fun of
you since you haven't sent me anything! You're so

SECRETIVE! LOL! But seriously, you can TOTALLY send me something! I want to be helpful! PLUS, I'm going to send you the rest of my story SOON too!

Kennedy ☺

From: Arthur Bean (arthuraaronbean@gmail.com)
To: Kennedy Laurel (imsocutekl@hotmail.com)
Sent: January 15, 17:03

Wow, Kennedy!

It sounds like your story gets better every week. I love the new twist! It reminds me of that thing that Shakespeare talked about — a dream within a dream — but I think your version is way cooler.

My story outline is still pretty rough. I'm just torn over what story to go forward with. I have so many stories almost done, but I don't know which to finish first. Anyway, maybe you could help me choose one.

Here is a list of my story ideas:

1) There is a boy who is the going to be the King, but he is too small to do anything and he is really poor. He meets a wizard who is living backwards in time, and he trains the boy to become the greatest king of all time. Then the wizard ends up getting stuck in time, but the boy becomes the King anyway because he finds the sword of the True King, and then leads a really great army and falls in love with a beautiful woman who becomes queen.

2) There is a boy who lives in a society that doesn't have any memories, but he becomes the Memory

Keeper for everyone in their village. He learns that his parents are part of the group of people who are making sure that no one has any memories. Then he finds out terrible things about the community and has to do something to change it.

3) There is a land over the stars where everything is very magical. A boy who lives there is the leader of a group of orphan boys and he can fly. He leaves the land and comes to New York. He meets a girl and her brothers and they have adventures with the boy. They meet pirates and mermaids and lions that can talk and stuff. They love being there, but then they realize that they would rather be at home with their parents, so after fighting with the evil guys on the island they end up flying home and being happy.

4) There are these pirate aliens that take over spaceships and then make the people in them do different things. But everyone in the spaceship gets old really fast and then they die. They don't know what to do so they go to Earth and get in the bodies of the grandparents. And then there's this change in the old people and they become really happy and energetic all the time, and they start to play like kids. They take over the playgrounds, and the kids get mad. So the kids go to the elves that live under the bridge in the city and they want to get their playground back. But the elves are fighting with dragons outside the city, so they need to get the giants on their side of the fight. But the kids don't know that the dragons exist so they decide to get the dragons to help them fight the grandparents. But the grandparents all disappear and get on the alien spaceship, but they don't have enough oxygen to go back to their planet

so they stay floating just above the city. So one boy who doesn't have parents realizes that the spaceship has his grandparents in it because he lives with his grandparents. Then he finds the giants and they fight the aliens, and they win. And the grandparents go back to being themselves, but they have to share their houses with the giants because the giants won the war. And then they all have to get used to having a giant living in their house.

5) Maybe something about racism.

I'd love your feedback on which one you think would be best.

Yours truly,
Arthur Bean

From: Kennedy Laurel (imsocutekl@hotmail.com)
To: Arthur Bean (arthuraaronbean@gmail.com)
Sent: January 16, 10:59

Hi Arthur!

You have so many ideas!!! And they are all so complicated! It's like you have the whole plot of *The Hobbit* trilogy or something!
I don't want to be super harsh, but um . . . they are pretty big plans! All of them sound like you could write like 100,000 pages on them and still not be done! A couple of them sound like other things too. Isn't your second idea the same story we studied in grade six? And I think your first idea is the same story

as King Arthur, and idea three is a lot like Peter Pan. NO OFFENCE! Maybe I'm reading something into them! And I don't even know what happened in your last idea!! There's like 8000 plots in that one!

As your creative writing partner, I just wanted to point that out. I don't want you to get accused of cheating later! I may want to win, but I don't want you to get kicked out as my competition LOL! ANYWAY, I always hear people say we should write about stuff we know about. Maybe you should try something more realistic. PLUS, you are so funny! You could totally win with a hilarious story about your cousin George or something!

Just a couple of thoughts from your FAVOURITE writing partner LOL!

Kennedy ☺

From: Arthur Bean (arthuraaronbean@gmail.com)
To: Kennedy Laurel (imsocutekl@hotmail.com)
Sent: January 16, 15:29

Dear Kennedy,

Thanks. I will think about it. But George doesn't really do much. Whenever I see him, he's just listening to his iPod on huge headphones. He barely speaks, actually. My cousin Luke (George's brother) told me the other day that George spent the entire weekend reorganizing his DVD collection. Literally, all weekend. I don't think that would make a great story.

Yours truly,
Arthur Bean

▶▶   ▶▶   ▶▶

Interview with Robbie Zack

I interviewed Robert Zack. Here is what we talked about, and which can be proven through a recording.

Arthur: What is your name?

Robbie: [doesn't say anything]

Arthur: How old are you?

Robbie: [doesn't say anything, but if you listen to the tape, you can hear him burp in my face]

Arthur: Do you like reading?

Robbie: No.

Arthur: Do you like writing?

Robbie: No it's boring.

Arthur: Then where do you get your ideas for your stories in English class?

Robbie: Why? Do you want to steal them?

Arthur: Were you born a jerk? Or is your jerk-ness just because you like being a jerk?

Robbie: Were you always a copycat nerd? Or did you copy that from your mom?

Arthur: My mom's dead. Jerk.

Robbie: As if.

Arthur: It's true. She died last year.

Robbie: Oh.

End of interview.

Arthur,

I believe you can do better than this. I would like you to redo the assignment, and think carefully about some better questions. I know that you can find some common interests and values between you and Robbie. It is tricky when you find yourself talking about a difficult subject, but try and recognize that Robbie didn't know about your mother passing away. You two may have difficulties communicating with each other, but a little understanding of someone else's situation can go a long way. Please submit your new assignment to me tomorrow.

Ms Whitehead

▶▶ ▶▶ ▶▶

Robbie Zack Interview: Take Two

Here is the written version of my second interview with Robbie Zack. I recorded it again, in case you don't believe me.

Arthur: What is your favourite colour?

Robbie: Red.

Arthur: What is your favourite subject?

Robbie: Drama.

Arthur: What is your least favourite subject?

Robbie: English.

Arthur: Ms Whitehead said that you have to cooperate and do my interview.

Robbie: I am. That's not even a question.

Arthur: But you're making it suck. You're only answering with one-word answers.

Robbie: Yep.

Arthur: Fine.

Robbie: Fine.

Arthur: I'm going to fail this assignment and it will be your fault.

Robbie: Impossible. You never fail anything. You've always been good at school.

Arthur: Because I do my homework. Do you even do your homework?

Robbie: There's no point. I'm probably going to suck at it anyway.

Arthur: Can't your mom help you?

Robbie: [doesn't say anything]

Arthur: Well?

Robbie: No. I'm out of here.

Then Robbie left. I don't think you can fail me for this, Ms Whitehead.

▸▸ ▸▸ ▸▸

Arthur,

I know you're having trouble with this assignment, but I really feel that you can succeed. Mr. Everett tells me that you're one of his best newspaper journalists, so I'm sure you can come up with great interview questions. I've spoken to Robbie as well, and I'd like you to try one more time to connect with Robbie in your interview. It's so important for famous writers to be able to create very diverse characters in their stories, and it's clear you and Robbie are very different! You can take some time during class today to complete the assignment.

Ms Whitehead

Robbie Zack Interview: Take Three

Arthur: I was told that I have to interview you again with better questions.

Robbie: I was told that I have to give you better answers, so let's get it over with.

Arthur: Good idea. First question: What kinds of stuff do you do for fun?

Robbie: Normal stuff. I don't know. Video games are my favourite, but I'm not allowed to play the good ones. I like Minecraft best. I like watching action movies. I play basketball sometimes. And soccer. I suck, but I still like it.

Arthur: You like movies. Is that why Drama is your favourite subject?

Robbie: I don't know. I guess so. It's good I guess because . . . I don't know . . . I guess there are fun people in the class. And it's not hard . . . It's good because you get to do whatever and like, fool around, like when I was a kid, but for marks, and then Mr. Tan says that it's creative. It's like we're just pretending stuff that's not true, but it feels like more than that sometimes. Which is way better than doing real stuff, you know?

Arthur: But your "real stuff" isn't hard. You just got back from Hawaii. Going to Hawaii for Christmas isn't hard. What's hard about your life?

Robbie: Lots of stuff. Just because I went to Hawaii doesn't mean that life isn't hard, you know. You think you're the only one with hard stuff and that makes you think you're better than other people.

Arthur: I don't think that I'm special. You don't understand. Your mom isn't dead.

Robbie: No, but she might as well be. She's moving away to North Carolina without us. My dad is moving my brother and me into some ugly townhouse and we have to share a bedroom. Life sucks.

Arthur: Oh.

Robbie: Yeah.

Arthur: Um, my next question is, What kind of books do you like to read?

Robbie: I told you that I don't like to read. Well I like comics. Do comics count?

Arthur: I guess so? I don't know. Maybe not.

Robbie: They should.

Arthur: I don't think so. They're just pictures.

Robbie: No way, man. The drawings add way more to the story because the artists are really good. Like this one about zombies? It's awesome. And it's not like all zombies are bad or nothing. They have personalities that have to be drawn in and all of them look different and you can spend hours looking at all the details on one page. You should read one. I bet you that you like it.

Arthur: I doubt that.

Robbie: I bet you will. I'm going to bring you one and then you have to read it.

Arthur: Fine. I'll read it, but I don't think I'll like it.

Robbie: Fine.

Arthur: Last question. Um, do you like knitting?

Robbie: Knitting? Like, sweaters?

Arthur: Or scarves or stuff. I mean, you can knit anything.

Robbie: That's the stupidest question I've ever heard.

End of interview.

Much better, Arthur. I'm glad to see that you and Robbie were able to work together on this assignment, and I hope you learned something too!

Ms Whitehead

▶▶ ▶▶ ▶▶

January 19th

Dear RJ,

Today was so hard! Ms Whitehead made me do
my homework like fourteen times! Well, three
times, but still. It felt like fourteen. And then
because of that, I was late to get to the cafeteria
for lunch and I missed out on the pizza they had
today. Plus, I saw Kennedy and I was just about to
say hello, and then all her friends were there and I
chickened out. Well, I mean, not really "chickened
out." It was just not the right time, because I didn't
want her friends to hear us talking. I mean, her
friend Catie makes a big deal out of EVERYTHING.
Anyway, I was all ready to ask her about the
Drama Club and how she liked it (even though I
already know), and then she would get excited and
start talking and then we would sit down together
to eat lunch and talk about all the stuff we have in
common, and it was going to be awesome, and she
was going to realize how cool I am.

I wonder if Robbie has been telling her that he
thinks I'm a geek. I know he thinks so, because
I've never played Minecraft. And I've never been
to Hawaii either. I mean, it sucks that he went
because his parents were getting divorced, but
the only place I went when Mom died was my
grandparents' house in Balzac. And there's
definitely no palm trees in Balzac. In fact, there's
nothing in Balzac. Seriously. Nothing.

Yours truly,
Arthur Bean

Hiya, Arthur,

As you know, there is an assembly coming up to celebrate the football team's league championship. How about you take a run at some event/sports writing for the newspaper? I bet you can cover the whole nine yards in one article!

Mr. E.

ALL THE WORLD'S A STAGE . . .
AND YOU CAN BE ON IT!!

The Drama Club is holding auditions for their spring production of *Romeo and Juliet*. No acting experience necessary; just come and join us on January 24th after school. Bring your flair for the dramatic, your angry soul, your romantic heart or your funniest class clown; there are roles for everybody! Maybe you will be the next big movie star: get your start now!

▶▶ ▶▶ ▶▶

January 20th

Dear RJ,

I had a dream last night that I was Romeo in the school play, and Kennedy was Juliet. It was glorious! We kissed and held hands, and everyone who saw the play said things like "You two have such chemistry!" and "You two make the most adorable couple!" Then Kennedy said, "Well, it wasn't acting, you know," and then she kissed me again, but not on stage. It was perfect.

I wish this was real. Then Kennedy would become a famous actress and we would get married. Then we would be this super famous couple, and after a while we would write a cookbook because we are secretly gourmet cooks.

So now I have to practise. Only four days until the auditions!

Yours truly,
Arthur Bean

Football Celebration Kicks Off on Wrong Foot

By Arthur Bean

Terry Fox Jr. High's assembly celebrating the victorious football team ended in tragedy yesterday when Katy Lamontagne, a popular grade nine student and girlfriend of Ryan Riker, was dropped from the top of a human pyramid and rushed to the hospital.

This show of carelessness and negligence is not the first for the accident-prone cheerleading squad of Terry Fox Jr. High. An unnamed source said that one cheerleader hit herself on the head with a baton during practice back in September. At the semi-final game against Lester B. Pearson Jr. High in November, another cheerleader threw up after spinning in the half-time number. To get to the bottom of these so-called accidents, this reporter interviewed Mr. Fringali, Gym teacher and junior team football coach.

When asked about the suspicious nature of the fall, Mr. Fringali said that there is always a risk of unbalance in the human pyramid, but that the squad had practised the move often. "It's not the girls' fault," said

Fringali. "They work very hard and are devastated by the severity of Katy's accident."

When pressed for more details about the weight distribution of the pyramid, Fringali would not comment, stating that the question was "rude" and "uncalled for." The only thing this reporter thinks is rude is the blatant cover-up of information from the school. Clearly there is something going on behind the scenes with this group of girls, and no one is talking about what it is. Maybe there is a broken mirror in their change room, or perhaps an unlucky rabbit's foot being carried around. One thing is for certain: this reporter will get to the bottom of this unlucky pyramid. The people want to know!

Hiya, Arthur,

An interesting take on the football celebration assembly! You must read a lot of detective novels! However, the thing is, I'm not too comfortable focusing on conspiracy theories surrounding the cheerleading squad. I've asked Robbie to add to your article with some of his photos and great captions from the rest of the celebration, and we'll use the first part of your article in the feature. Don't worry though; you and Robbie will be sharing the by-line on the article. Unless, of course, you want to stay undercover and use a pen name, in case the Feds are watching . . .

Mr. E.

▶▶ ▶▶ ▶▶

Peer Tutoring Program — Progress Report
Session: January 21st
Worked On: Shakespeare

Since we didnt have anything to work on, Artie
and I practissed the fight senes in the play for
the odditions for *Romeo and Juliet* next week.
— Robbie

"Wisely and slow; they stumble that run fast."
In case you were wondering, that's a quote from
Romeo and Juliet.
— Arthur

▶▶ ▶▶ ▶▶

Assignment: Interview About Me

Some of the best characters can be ourselves, so this assignment isn't even that much work for you! I would like you to interview someone who is close to you about a great subject: you! Please use at least five of the questions we brainstormed in class, and write out their answers using the same format as the last assignment. Of course, please avoid putting your friends or family in an awkward position by asking difficult or negative questions.

Due: January 25

▶▶ ▶▶ ▶▶

January 23rd

Dear RJ,

I need to confess something. I don't have a story. I have a lot of story beginnings. I even have a few story endings, but I can't get them to make a whole story.

I don't know what to do! I know I can do it. In elementary school, my teachers all said my stories were great. They said that I'm super creative, and that I would definitely be a famous author one day. So by now I should be able to write the best things ever, but I can't. Teachers shouldn't be allowed to tell you that you're great at something. It just makes life harder.

The stupid thing is that I know I can do it, I just don't know where to start. And then something comes up in life and I get stuck thinking about that. Like today. Today would have been my parents' anniversary, so I was thinking about how my mom always sent me to Nicole's house, and my parents would go out somewhere fancy for dinner that I wouldn't

102

like, like a seafood place or something like that.
Instead, Dad is sitting on the couch watching
TV and ignoring the phone that keeps ringing.
I answered it once and it was Luke's mom
calling to talk to him, but he only talked to her
for a second before he said he was going to call
her right back. And he never did. I called Luke
though, and we talked for an hour. He said that
he has Minecraft, so we can play it next time we
see each other. Who knows when that will be
though? It feels like forever sometimes. Auntie
Deborah said she was going to come down on her
own, but I hope she brings Luke. He could go to
my school for a while too. Although he might be
bored there. I think he thinks I'm cooler than I
am. And what if Kennedy fell in love with Luke
instead of me? He is the cooler version of me.
Maybe it's better if Luke stays in Edmonton.

Anyway, RJ, it feels like every week I
think that there won't be something to be sad
about, but then there's always SOMETHING,
like pizza night on Friday, or Christmas, or
Pancake Tuesday. Then I get stuck and can't
write about happy things. Sometimes I take
ideas and stuff from other places and try and
go from there, but it never works. I just want
one thing in my life to be perfect. And the only
thing that could be perfect is my writing. Is
that asking too much?

Yours truly,
Arthur Bean

▶▶ ▶▶ ▶▶

JUNIOR AUTHORS CONTEST

There is just over two months before the deadline for short story submissions on April 1. Your stories should already be completed in first draft, so use these final months to polish your work. Editing is key to a good story, so put your creative writing partners to work; don't forget that they will be working on their own stories too.

Don't leave things to the last minute; two months can go by very quickly!

Happy writing!

▶▶ ▶▶ ▶▶

Assignment: Interview About Me

By Arthur Bean

I asked my next door neighbour Nicole to answer some questions about me for this assignment. Here is what we talked about.

Arthur: When did you meet me and what was your first impression?

Nicole: I met you and your parents six years ago when I moved in. You were really small for your age. I remember that you ran around the courtyard a lot while singing Frank Sinatra songs and pretending to be an airplane. That was weird. Then I started babysitting you, and you liked to watch cartoons right before bed, and then read a book that was almost the same as the movie and compare them. It was cute.

Arthur: What are some of the things that I do best?

Nicole: Well, you're a pretty good knitter, especially

since you just started learning. You're good at talking to strangers when I have people over and you're here. You sure aren't shy! You like writing. You make a really good tomato sauce. You're pretty good about making your bed in the mornings. You always recycle.

Arthur: How likely is it that I will become a famous writer like Stephen King?

Nicole: Everything is possible if you work at it. But becoming a famous writer is really hard. You have to fail a lot to get there. Lots of people want to be writers, but they never get published. I think you have to work at lots of jobs in order to become a writer. Then it gives you lots to write about!

Arthur: What can I do better in life?

Nicole: You're only twelve . . .

Arthur: I'm thirteen.

Nicole: Only thirteen. You've got plenty of time to screw up your life in ways you can't even imagine yet. Trust me! I say keep doing what you're doing, and everything will work out for the best.

Arthur: No. I mean right now.

Nicole: Oh. Well, you could clean up the kitchen more often. Your dishes are always left in the sink for way longer than a day. It's gross.

Arthur: Thank you, Nicole.

Nicole: You're welcome, Arthur.

Arthur, your babysitter Nicole is very astute! I hope you found this assignment useful.

Kennedy mentioned that you're having trouble with your story for the competition. If you wish to speak with me about it, I'd be happy to meet with you after class. Sometimes all we need is someone to talk through our challenges in order to get them down on paper!

Ms Whitehead

Dear Ms Whitehead,

Nicole is not my babysitter. She is my next door neighbour who I spend time with when my dad is home late from work. Sometimes I see her socially also because she is teaching me to knit. She is my friend. This is a big difference from babysitter. A babysitter is for people like Robbie, who probably needs constant supervision or else he would likely burn his house down.

Also, I'm not having any trouble with my story. Kennedy made a mistake there. I don't know why she would say that, because it's totally not true. I don't need any help figuring out my ideas. I'm almost finished my story and I feel confident that it's great.

Yours truly,
Arthur Bean

Arthur,

Good to hear that things are going well. I look forward to reading your story in its finished form. Don't forget to double space your work!

Ms Whitehead

▶▶ ▶▶ ▶▶

CAST LIST: *Romeo and Juliet*

DIRECTOR: Mr. Tan
STAGE MANAGER: Amelia Lewis
ASSISTANT STAGE MANAGER: Robert Zack
ROMEO: Arthur Bean
JULIET: Kennedy Laurel
NURSE: Benjamin Crisp
MERCUTIO: Curtis Westleigh
BENVOLIO: Latha Nantikarn
TYBALT: Andrew Brock
CHORUS AND OTHERS: Surya Hatta, Gemma Hemming, Tom McAulista, Liam Wilson, Sierra Barthes, Taylor Van Den Furthe, Mai Nguyen, Cristal-Leigh St. Jean-Adams, Phil Topor, Von Ipo, Audrey Eng, Taylor Tom, Fiona Chong, Ezra Galen
UNDERSTUDY ROMEO: Robert Zack
UNDERSTUDY JULIET: Audrey Eng

▶▶ ▶▶ ▶▶

January 27th

Dear RJ,

I got it!!! I'm going to be Romeo and Kennedy's going to be Juliet!! We get to kiss and everything! We will be the two greatest lovers of all time. I know it! The chemistry between us is so strong. I bet that Mr. Tan could feel the chemistry between us in class and knew that we would be perfect as R&J! It will be so easy to be Romeo. I think that I might be as good an actor as I am a writer. It will probably be pretty hard for me to choose how I want to be famous later. I bet they will turn my books into movies and famous directors will ask me to star as my characters. Of course, I will have work at memorizing the lines. I am not very good at memorizing stuff. But still! A kiss, forsooth!

Yours truly,
Arthur Bean

▸▸ ▸▸ ▸▸

From: Arthur Bean (arthuraaronbean@gmail.com)
To: Kennedy Laurel (imsocutekl@hotmail.com)
Sent: January 28, 10:30

Dear Kennedy,

Congratulations on your role in the play! I'm so happy for you, and I think we will make a great lead couple, don't you? I can't wait for rehearsals to start. Maybe we can meet this weekend and start practising together. My friend Nicole says they call it "running scenes" in "the biz." I'm pretty free since we had a substitute in Math on Friday — no homework for the weekend!

Yours truly,
Arthur Bean

From: Kennedy Laurel (imsocutekl@hotmail.com)
To: Arthur Bean (arthuraaronbean@gmail.com)
Sent: January 28, 12:05

Hi Arthur!

Congratulations to you too!!! I'm SO excited to play Juliet! It will be my first big break in show biz LOL! Maybe my EX-boyfriend will see us kiss and get jealous LOL! I can't "run scenes" (look at us, talking like theatre pros LOL) this weekend. I've got a volleyball tournament! But once we know what Mr. Tan has in store for rehearsals, we can maybe find a noon hour where we can practise! That is, in the midst of writing award-winning stories, hard-hitting journalism and all that HOMEWORK LOL!

Also, have you talked to Robbie? He's pretty bummed about not getting the role of Romeo ☹ He was soooo into the Drama class, and I think he's really good at acting too. Anyway, if you talk to him soon, be extra nice to him. He was so sad on the way home. He came over yesterday and we made popcorn and watched Jim Carrey movies. They were so dumb, but so funny!

Off to WIN a volleyball competition LOL!!

Kennedy ☺

From: Arthur Bean (arthuraaronbean@gmail.com)
To: Kennedy Laurel (imsocutekl@hotmail.com)
Sent: January 28, 12:21

Dear Kennedy,

Actually, I'm glad you can't make it. I'd forgotten that I'm actually really busy this weekend too. I have all kinds of activities to attend and a party as well. But we'll totally have to reschedule for a time when we are both free!

   I don't think Robbie was that interested in getting a part; he was probably just upset for a minute. I think being an understudy is a pretty big thing, and assistant stage manager is also really important. Like Mr. Tan said . . . no part is too small!

   Good luck at your volleyball tournament!

Yours truly,
Arthur Bean

FEBRUARY

Assignment: Dramatic Scenes

Conversations can be tricky in story writing, and writers often have trouble moving a story forward using dialogue instead of description. After looking at scenes of plays today in class, please use these works as inspiration for your own short play! Write a short scene for a play where two characters meet and solve a problem together. These characters can be real people from your life, based on previous assignments, or new characters who share personality traits with people you've met, or even yourself! Try and weave these details into the conversation seamlessly; don't just come out and tell your reader directly. Your scene should be at least two pages long, double-spaced.

Due: February 4

▶▶   ▶▶   ▶▶

**Peer Tutoring Program — Progress Report
Session: February 2nd
Worked On: Dramatic Scenes**

Ms Whitehead, I suggest that Robbie see someone for his violent tendencies in his work. Seriously, that guy has some issues that need to be worked out, and I am afraid that he might kill me the same way his "character" kills me in his scene. I doubt that I will sleep well tonight.
— Arthur Bean

Artie helped me with my sene, to make one of
the caracters responsable for the problem. The
problem is that one of them is staring in the play
and the other one wants to star to. Together they
kill the other star and never get caught. It's pretty
funny. I also got to use the word "cleave"— like
"to cleave someone's head open with an axe."
— Robbie

▶▶ ▶▶ ▶▶

February 3rd

Dear RJ,

Today we had our first read-through of *Romeo
and Juliet*. It was so great. Now Mr. Tan wants
us to rehearse scene by scene. He said that
it's best if we can find the driving emotion (he
called it the character's motivation) and act
that. He said that it is best if we relate that
emotion to something in our own lives and write
about it in our notebooks. I drew a picture of
a heart with a bloody sword sticking through
it on the cover of mine, with an empty poison

bottle next to the heart. I think it will remind me of the tragedy of the play each time I see it.

I can't wait until we get to the part where I get to kiss Kennedy, though. I bet her lips are super soft, because she uses a lot of lip gloss. I just wish I got to work with only her, but Mr. Tan said that we were going to rehearse with Audrey and Robbie there too, since they "need to know the blocking," where you have to stand on stage for each scene. (It's very technical.) But it's so crowded when there's four of us trying to do everything. Plus, I got paired with Robbie on this other drama scene in class. Why do I always have to work with him? Is there a conspiracy against me?

Yours truly,
Arthur Bean

▶▶ ▶▶ ▶▶

Assignment: Dramatic Scene

CAST LIST: Nancy, a girl
                     Darian, a boy

Nancy: Hey! Hey, you there! Who are you?

Darian: I'm Darian. I live down the street. We just moved here from Ohio. My parents are getting divorced.

Nancy: OK. Can you help me with my problem?

Darian: Maybe. What is your problem?

Nancy: I'm trying to get my little sister out of the sewer.

Darian: How did you sister end up in the sewer?

Nancy: That's a long story.

Darian: I've got time. My parents are divorced, and I don't know anyone here yet since I just moved from Ohio.

Nancy: Well, I put her in the sewer. She was annoying me. She keeps repeating everything I say.

[From below the stage]: She keeps repeating everything I say.

Nancy: SHUT UP!

[From below the stage]: Shut up!

Nancy: I MEAN IT!

[From below the stage]: I mean it!

Darian: Are you sure you want to get her out? She seems pretty happy down there. She should be fine as long as she doesn't see a crocodile.

Nancy: Do you think there are crocodiles down there?

Darian: I know there are. I'm super smart. I learned about crocodiles that live in the sewers. They can grow to be up to 25 feet long.

Nancy: How long is that in metres?

Darian: I don't know. I'm from Ohio.

Nancy [yelling down the sewer]: Do you hear that, Franklina? There are crocs down there! You had better be quiet in case they can find you using sonar tracking like bats use!

Darian: So how do you think we should get your sister out of the sewer?

Nancy: Well, I knitted this scarf.

Darian: You can knit? That's the coolest thing I have ever heard. You must be really cool. My friend Arthur in Ohio could knit too, and he was the greatest person to ever live.

Nancy: He sounds dreamy. Maybe instead of getting my sister out of the sewer, I should move to Ohio and marry your friend Arthur.

Darian: You had better move soon. He's going to be very famous soon because he's a really great writer too. He's going to write the next bestselling novel.

Nancy: I will give him this scarf, and make him spaghetti and meatballs, even though I am a vegetarian. But since I love him so much, I will still make meatballs for him.

Darian: I am a vegetarian too!

Nancy: We have so much in common! We are both vegetarians, and we both think Arthur is the greatest!

Darian: Maybe you should stay here.

Nancy: No. I have to go to Ohio. You could come too, and live with your mom.

Darian: OK. I like Ohio.

[Nancy and Darian leave]

[Voice from below]: Hello?

[Screaming and the sound of a girl being eaten by a crocodile.]

The End

Arthur,

Your interpretation of the assignment
is very imaginative. However, most of
your character description is still being
told through your characters' exposition,
and you abandon your "problem" of
the sister in the sewer in the middle
of your scene. I'm also not certain
what character traits you are trying
to portray in your characters. Keep
working on blending personality traits
into your work. Remember, SHOW the
readers something, don't TELL them!

Ms Whitehead

▶▶ ▶▶ ▶▶

February 5th

Dear RJ,

I don't suppose you have written any stories
for me HAHAHA. I know that's asking a lot,
especially since you are an inanimate object.
But seriously, RJ, enough with the jokes. I've
really got to write a story. Once I start I won't
be able to stop writing. The words will just
flow from my fingers onto the page. I probably
won't even have to edit it much. It's just that I
can't get my fingers going! Plus, I have all these
rehearsals too. It's very tricky to write my own
words when I'm trying to memorize someone
else's.

I tried asking Nicole for ideas and she said
that I should write about a sad rabbit making

friends with other animals in the forest. It was the stupidest idea ever. I told her that and she got offended and said that a great allegory is often the simplest story. Then I had to look up *allegory*, and I think she was making fun of me. Whatever. She's not trying to be a great writer. I am.

Yours truly,
Arthur Bean

▶▶ ▶▶ ▶▶

Romeo and Juliet — a Star's Reflection

By Arthur Bean

Act 1, Scenes 1 and 2
In this first scene, I play a man in love. And oh! What a love it is! It is intense and passionate. I imagine myself like I am a fire, and I have been doused in gasoline. I burn and burn and burn!

(Is this what you mean, Mr. Tan? I'm not sure what I'm supposed to be doing in this reflection journal.)

Romeo/Arthur,

You're on the right track and I'd like to see more emotion. Really feel what Romeo is feeling . . . Is Romeo really in love in this scene? How does he feel about being in love? Is he happy about it? Does it make him sad? Does it make him angry? Read over your lines, and

117

try and find something in your life that helps you connect with how Romeo is feeling. It can be a memory or present-day feelings . . . Don't hold back; Romeo is very dramatic, but he is also very nuanced!

Mr. Tan

A ROSE BY ANY OTHER NAME . . .

Help support the Drama Department's costume fund by buying a rose for your Valentine! Roses will be on sale in the cafeteria at lunch hour every day this week.
Cost: $2 a rose
Show someone you care! Two colours available!
Red Roses: True Love. Pink Roses: Secret Admirer
All roses will be delivered on February 14th during sixth period.

February 7th

Dear RJ,

I'm going to talk to Kennedy at school tomorrow. Not just in class or in rehearsal, but at lunch or something. I'm going to do it. Something light and funny to remind her of how funny I am. I can't decide if I should get her a rose for Valentine's Day either. I think that maybe if I start just talking to her then maybe she will send me a rose! This is the first time

on Valentine's Day where Valentines count.
In my elementary school we always had to
give a Valentine to everyone in the class. Then
everyone would count up their cards to see
who got the most. Big reveal, RJ: It was never
me. Somehow I never got as many as the other
kids in my class, even though it was a rule
that you had to give one to everyone. I guess
not everyone played by the rules. I sure didn't.
I mean, I never gave one to Robbie or any of
his friends. My mom made me write them out,
and would keep track to make sure I did the
whole class, but I threw out the ones for kids I
didn't like on my way to school. But this year
they mean something! And you never know,
RJ, maybe I'll get a secret admirer rose from
someone!

Ha! That would be awesome, but I doubt it.
Kennedy doesn't know that she loves me yet. I
just like to pretend sometimes as if she does. It's a
lot easier than doing anything else. For example,
right now, I should be writing my story for the
competition. But I don't feel like it. Every time I
come home, I have these really great intentions
to get something done, but it seems as though
walking through the door sucks all the energy out
of me to do anything. This weekend I tried to get
my dad to go to the movies with me, but he gave
me money to go alone and said, "Not really feeling
it, buddy." I could have gone, but who goes to the
movies by themselves? Instead I went to the wool
store with Nicole and listened to her talk about
dating with her friends who work there. It was so
boring. Girl talk is so boring.

And the whole time we were there I felt guilty for not writing. Nicole says that even when you're procrastinating, you're thinking about the project you're putting off. But it's not true. I think about anything *but* that.

Yours truly,
Arthur Bean

▶▶ ▶▶ ▶▶

Peer Tutoring Program — Progress Report
Session: February 9th
Worked On: Romeo and Juliet

Ms W: Artie fixed my speling on a comic strip for the r&j journal mr t is making us keep. Like we didn't have enuf homework . . .
— Robbie

Ms Whitehead, it's weird that Robbie can make a comic strip out of pretty much anything. Did you know that he can do that?
— Arthur Bean

▶▶ ▶▶ ▶▶

JUNIOR AUTHORS CONTEST

REMINDER: All entries are due for the Junior Authors Contest on April 1st! Please submit your stories to your English teacher directly, or to the office. All stories must have a title page with your full name, your teacher's name, and your class in the right-hand corner.

Example:

John Doe
Mrs. Ireland
Class 8B

Good luck, everyone!

▶▶ ▶▶ ▶▶

Hiya, Arthur,

I've got an assignment for you, Romeo! Can you tap into your inner romantic, and cover the poetry reading for the paper? Mrs. Ireland's grade eight English class will be performing their poems in the Drama room, and it sounded like an event that's right up your alley.

Cheers!
Mr. E.

P.S.: Why couldn't the poet get a bank loan? Because he already "ode" too much!

▶▶ ▶▶ ▶▶

February 12th

Dear RJ,

Another week gone, and still no story and no girlfriend. I was going to talk to Kennedy this week. I really was. But then I found the sequel to *The Hitchhiker's Guide to the Galaxy* in the library so I read that over lunch hour sometimes, and then I was helping Mr. Everett with the newspaper layout a couple of times, and I had rehearsal and I have so many lines to learn! I mean, I really was going to do it, RJ. I really was! I was just so busy!

About Kennedy. OK. Fine. I chickened out. I mean, I did read in the library, and I did practise my lines, but I definitely chickened out. It's so hard to talk to her when all her

friends are around! Plus, I think her friend
Catie doesn't like me at all. She's one of those
girls who seems really nice, but I've seen her
say something to me, and then when she thinks
I'm not watching, she whispers something to
her friend and they giggle a lot. So I didn't say
anything. Next week though. I'm going to make
a move next week.

I talked to Luke today too about getting story
ideas. He said that he would think about it and
let me know if he had some. I told him my title
idea. I thought I would call it "The Darkness
of the Soul." It sounds so dramatic. I don't
know what it will be about, but Luke thought it
sounded pretty versatile.

It actually sounds kind of like it could
describe my dad a little bit. Luke said that his
mom is really worried about my dad. It was
weird. I guess I hadn't really thought about
him. I mean, I know he's sad about my mom,
but I didn't think that I had to worry about
him. I mean, he's the grown-up. He should be
more worried about me than me about him. Not
that he has to worry about me. I have so many
things to do I don't even have time to be sad all
the time!

Yours truly,
Arthur Bean

▸▸ ▸▸ ▸▸

From: Kennedy Laurel (imsocutekl@hotmail.com)
To: Arthur Bean (arthuraaronbean@gmail.com)
Sent: February 14, 22:34

Hi Arthur!!

Happy Valentine's Day!! Did you have a good day??
I had a wonderful day!! I got TWO roses at school!
One was RED and the other was PINK!!! I have a
secret admirer LOL!!

AND the impossible happened! Sandy came to
my house after school, and told me that he had
sent the red rose, and asked me to be his girlfriend
again!!!!!!!!! OF COURSE I said YES LOL!!! It was
soooo romantic! It was like a movie or something!! I
was starting to think that he didn't care anymore, but
then I thought maybe his poem at the poetry reading
was about me but I didn't want to seem conceited
or anything but then it WAS about me!! It's so
awesome!!! BEST VALENTINE'S DAY EVER!!! ☺

And then there's still the pink rose! Kayla said that
one of them HAD to be from you because you are SO
into your role as Romeo LOL!!! I told her that there
was NO WAY it was from you because the writing was
SO MESSY on the card, and you seem like the kind of
guy whose writing would be SO NEAT LOL!

ANYWAY, I just thought I would wish you a happy
Valentine's Day!! OK, I will see you in rehearsal
Monday! Oh, but I PROMISED Sandy that I wouldn't
kiss Romeo until the real show LOL! Otherwise he
would be so jealous LOL!!

Kennedy ☺

February 14th

Dear RJ,

I hate her! I hate Kennedy and I hate Sandy and I hate Valentine's Day and everything!

Why would she send me an email like that? What's her problem? Does she think I want to hear about her stupid boyfriend sending her a stupid rose and showing up on her stupid doorstep? I hate him. He thinks he's so romantic but he doesn't see how awesome Kennedy really is. He doesn't understand her. Kennedy is amazing. She is kind and smart and super talented and Sandy Dickason probably just dates her because she's pretty.

I don't get it! What does she see in him?? Doesn't she realize that I'm her soulmate? I do all the same things she does, and I like the same stuff, and I'm always there for her. Why doesn't she notice that? I KNEW I should have sent her a rose for Valentine's Day, but I thought that would be lame, and I wanted to do something more. I was going to knit her mittens, but now STUPID Sandy Dickason comes back and ruins everything! Stupid Sandy. Or should I say Stupid Arthur. I can't do anything right. I'll probably be alone forever.

Yours truly,
Arthur Bean

▶▶ ▶▶ ▶▶

Cupid Misses Mark During Poetry Reading

By Arthur Bean

Mrs. Ireland's grade eight English class performed original works they wrote for Valentine's Day in a noon hour poetry reading February 14th. The poems ranged from mushy to heartbroken to downright depressing. No one should be forced to sit through an hour of rhyming couplets that end with the words *heart* and *part*. I, for one, can think of one more word that rhymes with *heart*, and it smells about as good as most of the poetry at the reading. School events like this are excellent reasons as to why the lunch hour should be shortened to 30 minutes.

Of course, there were a few poems that stood out in the sea of banality. Daisy Yau's poem "Grandfather Clock" was simple and moving, capturing the love between granddaughter and grandfather. Amaya Hazmeet wrote and performed a ballad called "Heartbroken Annie." Although the lyrics were forced at times, her guitar playing was good and broke up the monotony of the poems. The worst poem award goes to Sandy Dickason for his poem titled "Love Is All Around My Heart." It's possible that this was plagiarized, because it sure sounded like it was written by a six year old. It is expected that he will be suspended for writing terrible poems.

Arthur,

Ouch! You're being a little harsh on the grade eight class! Remember that chat we had during the last layout session? We talked about being objective and not letting our feelings get in the way of our work. I think you're very creative,

Arthur, but your articles aren't up to the quality that I know you can do. I've asked Kennedy to write up something on the poetry reading that is more positive, and I need you to take a good look inside and decide if you really want to be part of the newspaper team. I'm happy to chat with you about anything you want, and I'm even here if you'd like to vent about something you didn't enjoy, but if you're going to continue with the newspaper, we need to work on developing objective writing skills (and biting our tongue when it's necessary).

Thanks, Arthur. I really do appreciate your sense of humour and creativity, and you've got a great work ethic!

Mr. E.
P.S.: What kind of flowers are the worst gifts on Valentine's Day? Cauliflowers!

▶▶ ▶▶ ▶▶

Romeo and Juliet — a Star's Reflection

By Romeo

Act 1, Scene 4

In this scene I have to be devious. It's important that I get into the party at Juliet's house, but they can't know that I am not invited. So I have to come up with a plan to sneak in. It's very sneaky. I don't know if it's the right idea or not, but I am pretty desperate to get into the greatest party of the century. We all have to do things that aren't morally right sometimes, to get ahead, and maybe Juliet *is* dating someone else right now, but I'm sure once she sees me at the party, she will fall in love with me instead of that other guy.

I know that it will all turn out right in the end. I'm sure of it. Because it has to, right? I am the hero, so things are going to work out for me, I think.

Your reflections are getting stronger, Arthur. Next time try focusing on something specific in your life, rather than being very general. Find the poetry in the everyday emotion . . . I think you will find it easier to fully immerse yourself in Romeo that way, rather than focusing on the action of the scene.
  Believe!

Mr. Tan

▶▶ ▶▶ ▶▶

February 20th

Dear RJ,

What a terrible week. All my teachers hate me. Even Mr. Everett, who is always super nice to me, was mean to me this week. It's his fault though. I'm just trying to be honest, and all he wants for the newspaper is puppies and kittens and sunshine. It's not true to life, RJ. I'm just telling it like it is.

I've been thinking about it all week, and I'm still so mad about Kennedy getting back together with Sandy. She's the one missing out. I'm smart. I'm nice. I'm fun. I'm going to be famous one day. I think she was trying to hurt me because she knows that I should win the story contest. I *should* win the story contest.

But I won't, will I, RJ? Because you need a story to win, not just a couple of ideas or a title. You know, I'll probably come in last place. Even Robbie will beat me, because his story ideas are good and he'll illustrate it or something. He'll probably win even though he said that he wouldn't enter the competition.

That's how much my life will suck then. As if it doesn't suck right now.

You know, RJ, other people don't understand what it's like to lose something really big in your life. People like Kennedy. She's one of those people where everything goes right in her life all the time. I HATE those people! And now I'm going to lose the contest and I guess I'll just add that to my list of lost things: my mom and my potential girlfriend and my future.

Yours truly,
Arthur Bean

▶▶ ▶▶ ▶▶

Peer Tutoring Program — Progress Report
Session: February 22nd
Worked On:

neither artie or me didnt want to do anything today so we didnt. then artie went home early anyway
— Robbie

▸▸ ▸▸ ▸▸

Assignment: Conflict

This week we studied conflict in short stories. There are different kinds of conflict:

1) Person versus Person: a conflict between your characters

2) Person versus Him/Herself: Your character has an internal struggle over what is right or wrong

3) Person versus Nature: Your character struggles against natural forces, such as an animal or the weather

4) Person versus Supernatural: Your character struggles with forces outside our Earth, like ghosts, aliens or werewolves, etc.

Think of a conflict that you have dealt with in your life and describe it. If you decide to use a conflict that is ongoing, create a good ending for your story from your imagination. Please underline the climax of your story, as we did for the other short stories we read in class.

Due: March 7

MARCH

Peer Tutoring Program — Progress Report
Session: March 1st
Worked On: Conflict

Artie helped me alot with my conflict
assignment for next week he said that it was
good he thought but hear it is anyway in case I
should change it.
— Robbie

My mom has a job. She travels alot for work.
She goes to the States alot and leaves me and
my brother at home with my dad who can only
cook omelets. One day my mom comes home
and says that she has a trip to North Carolina
for two weeks. She leaves for work but then her
sister (my aunt) gets into a car accident. My dad
tries to call my mom in North Carolina but she
is not staying at the hotel. She doesn't call back,
and finds out about her sister (my aunt) when
she comes home. My dad and her sister (my
aunt) are suspicious when she has a tan. My dad
and mom fight alot more.
    My mom's company gets downsized and she
loses her job. She cries alot but then she still
goes to North Carolina, and my dad gets really
mad about it. <u>My parents take my brother and
me to Hawaii to tell us that they are getting
a divorce.</u> My mom is now in love with a

salesman in North Carolina and is moving away. My dad cries alot, even though my dad never cries. My dad puts the house up for sale, but no one will buy it. We still live there, but my dad gets really nervous about finances and paying for stuff alone. We eat alot of omelets.

Ms Whitehead: Robbie still doesn't believe me that *a lot* is two words. You have to tell him. Other than that, you should probably give him an *A* on this. I think it's pretty dramatic.
— Arthur

▶▶ ▶▶ ▶▶

Conflict in My Life

By Arthur Bean

Arthur Bean goes to junior high and is surrounded by a bunch of new people. Arthur meets a girl in his Gym class. She is awesome at playing volleyball, but she is also nice to the people who can't play volleyball. She is very competitive too, and she swears at the other team when she loses her first game. Then she gets really embarrassed and apologizes to the class. Because she is honest, the teacher doesn't report her for swearing.

Arthur is paired with the volleyball girl for a city-wide writing competition. The volleyball girl wants to spend more time with Arthur, but his busy schedule doesn't allow him to see her very often. This upsets the volleyball girl, but Arthur has to do what he has to do for his art. The volleyball girl goes away at Christmas on a ski trip, but writes Arthur long love letters. <u>Arthur feels conflicted about entering the story contest because the volleyball girl's story will also be in the running for the best story.</u> However, he also knows that she is pretty nice, and shouldn't have to feel bad when he wins.

The volleyball girl falls madly in love with Arthur while rehearsing *Romeo and Juliet* and decides not to enter the competition so that Arthur can win the story contest. Instead, she decides to focus on becoming a famous actress and volleyball player.

Arthur is touched by the volleyball girl's generosity in stepping aside for his career. Since both of them are happy, Arthur gives in to her love for him and marries her.

Dear Arthur,

You failed to identify a real conflict <u>between</u> your characters. In a short story, the conflict should happen quickly to engage the reader. When we work on our short stories for class, try and make the inciting action the beginning of your conflict. I'm certain you have better real-life examples of conflict than this one!

Ms Whitehead

▶▶ ▶▶ ▶▶

133

Romeo and Juliet — a Star's Reflection

By Romeo

Act 2, Scene 4

In this scene I am considering changing my name, because then I will be happier with my true love. This is our first meeting where I get to speak to her, and it is both exciting and terrible. It is a happy encounter because I learn that Juliet feels the same way about me as I do about her. This reminds me of a time Kennedy wrote me an email telling me she was excited to be my partner in a writing group. I knew then that the universe had linked us to be soulmates. But it is also torture, because we can't be together.

This is kind of like the disappointment I feel when my cousins come to town, and we have a really fun time together, but then they leave. So I really like it when they visit, but then I'm really sad that they don't live closer to me so that we could hang out all the time. It's not romantic at all, but it definitely sucks in the same way that it sucks for Romeo that he can't be Juliet's boyfriend because their parents hate each other. Lucky for me, I don't think Kennedy's parents have ever met my dad. Not that they would hate him. He's a nice guy, but he's really quiet and doesn't do much. Maybe they would hate him for that. I doubt it though.

Beautiful work, Arthur. Such true emotions will be a powerful beacon for dramatization as we run through the scene . . . the best actors are able to direct their emotions through someone else's words. Now that you have tapped into something tied to your soul, try and use these things as your motivation to get to the end of the scene.

Mr. Tan

▸▸ ▸▸ ▸▸

Peer Tutoring Program — Progress Report
Session: March 9th
Worked On: Stuff

notheing to report
— Robbie

Ditto.
— Arthur Bean

▸▸ ▸▸ ▸▸

March 10th

Dear RJ,

BIG NEWS! It turns out ROBBIE ZACK was the guy who sent Kennedy the secret admirer rose! AS IF!

He told me today during tutoring! He kept making comments about this girl he liked and how she totally led him on and stuff. So finally I asked him what he was talking about, and he totally spilled the beans to the Bean (hahaha, that's a little name humour for you, RJ). So then he tells me about how his dad finally sold their house and they'll be moving, and Kennedy is too busy with her *boyfriend* to notice that he's moving to a whole other neighbourhood. Then he told me about sending her the rose but how his romantic gesture was lost because Sandy came back. It made me so glad that I didn't send her a rose too — mine would have been the same! Then he actually asked ME for advice. I didn't have any advice. I just told him that she was really nice and didn't mean to ignore him or something. But no WONDER he was upset about not getting to be Romeo!

You know, RJ, I can't tell if I feel bad for Robbie, or if I feel good about him feeling bad. I mean, I guess I should be more mad at him, because now we're in competition for the same girl, but there's no way he has a shot. I mean, he said he lived next door, so of course you're nice to the person who lives next door to you. I bet Kennedy thinks of him more like a brother. I actually think I maybe feel a little bit bad for the guy. I definitely know how he feels, but it must be worse for him, since he doesn't have any chance with her.

Yours truly,
Arthur Bean

▶▶ ▶▶ ▶▶

Assignment: Short Story

It's time to put together all the elements that we have studied lately and exercise our creativity by writing short stories! This major project is not due until June, so feel free to talk to me throughout the process. You can use any element of a previous assignment as your jumping-off point if you wish.

A few reminders:

Choose your protagonist and your point of view. Who is telling the story? Who is the story about?

Develop your characters. Make them real people with real problems.

Use dialogue. This helps develop your characters, and moves your story forward.

Pick a conflict. What is your character trying to achieve? What obstacles are in his or her way?

Resolve your story. Don't leave your reader hanging. Choose a plot line that is short enough to fit into a short story; I don't have time to mark thirty novels!

The hardest part about writing is getting started. Don't be daunted by a blank page; you can go back and fix things after you've started. Don't think; just write!

Don't leave your story until the last minute! I've given you a lot of time to work on it, and I hope you will use your time wisely and write an outline and a few drafts. A piece that is thrown together the weekend before the due date is easy to spot in a sea of polished stories.

Due: June 6

MS WHITEHEAD

We are sorry to announce that Ms Whitehead has broken her hip in a skiing accident this weekend and will not be at school for a few weeks. She is recovering comfortably at home, and is in good spirits despite the accident.

If any students would like to sign a get-well card for Ms Whitehead, please visit the office before Thursday.

▶▶ ▶▶ ▶▶

March 14th

Dear RJ,

I can't believe Ms Whitehead broke her hip! I knew she was older because only old people break their hips. But she can't be that old — she was skiing! She must be very fit for her age.

I feel bad for Ms Whitehead. I'll write something nice in the get-well card. I'm sure that will cheer her up.

I wonder if this means we don't have to turn in that short story assignment we just got.

Yours truly,
Arthur Bean

▶▶ ▶▶ ▶▶

Romeo and Juliet — a Star's Reflection

By Romeo

Act 2, Scene 3

In this scene I am debating whether Juliet really wants to be with me. I mean, REALLY wants to be with me. It seems that I am making all these plans for our future together, and all she does is talk to her nurse about stuff, and occasionally say nice things about me from her balcony. It's very infuriating. So I am sitting back and taking stock of what is really important. I know I love her, but does she love me back? She seems to be really into Mercutio instead. I mean, maybe she loves me in secret and that would be OK, but at some point she has to commit to being my girlfriend.

I think you misread this scene, Arthur. This is not quite what Romeo is doing in the play, and I'm not sure that he really ever questions Juliet's love in this manner. If you have any questions about the language Shakespeare uses, we can discuss it after rehearsal. I find it's best to read it with your heart, not your head. Trust in your soul!

Mr. Tan

▶▶ ▶▶ ▶▶

We will be continuing our active reading by discussing different techniques that can be used to keep the reader's interest. Please read the first short story in your anthology. After you're done, fill in some of your own reflections about the story on the worksheet and hand them in to Mrs. Carrell by the end of the period.

There will be no extensions given on this assignment. It is imperative that you use your class time effectively.

Arthur Bean

7A

"The Lake" Worksheet

1. Who is the protagonist of the story? How do you know?
The protagonist is the main character of the story. I know because he is the one the author talks about the most.

2. Where does the story take place? What is the time of year?
The story takes place on a farm, because all of the most boring Canadian stories take place on farms. This one is different because it takes place in the summer and Canadians normally only write about winter.

3. What is the mood of the story? How do you know?
The mood is quiet and sleepy. I know because I fell asleep reading it.

4. Describe the plot of the story in 3 to 5 sentences.
The main character Johnnie goes to the lake. He drops a ball in the lake and cries about it because his father is mean. Johnnie gets the ball out after thinking about it for a long time. He decides to leave the farm but he leaves the ball on his bed.

5. What is the theme of the story?
The theme of the story is that balls prefer sleeping to swimming.

6. Many authors use symbols in their stories. What do you think the ball symbolizes?
The ball symbolizes Johnnie's love for his father. It might symbolize the world, since it is also round. It could also symbolize how the author wants to drown himself because he knows that he is really boring and ruining the lives of students everywhere by writing the world's worst story.

Dear Ms Whitehead,

Mrs. Carrell is making me write you a letter to explain my answers on the worksheet. I explained to her that my best work is not done working in restricted space, and that I did the best I could answering the questions. It's not my fault that she reads my answers as being "impertinent" and "disrespectful to the learning process." I think that my answers to her worksheet show my creative thinking and my attempt to go above and beyond the exercise. At least when you were here we didn't just fill in the blanks on a stupid worksheet.

Get well soon.

Yours truly,
Arthur Bean

March 16th

Dear RJ,

I came up with a really great story idea! I'm thinking that my story will be about a snake tamer. He'll work for the circus as a snake trainer, and he'll have all these really dangerous snakes that work for him, and he can hypnotize them and stuff. He gets the snakes to commit a crime of some kind and then the circus goes on to the next town, so he's like a mastermind criminal and he decides to do something big or something. I don't know what will happen next, but I think it's a good start. I'm going to start writing it this weekend. It can be all mysterious and I can describe a lot of foggy nighttime scenes. This could be it, RJ! I think I've got a winner!

Yours truly,
Arthur Bean

▸▸ ▸▸ ▸▸

Since today is St. Patrick's Day, I thought we would write limericks in class. As you know, a limerick has a very specific rhyme scheme and syllable count. Marks will be awarded based on the adherence to the specifications of the limerick poem. Remember, the limerick is often a cheeky and fun poem, but this is a school classroom. I don't want to see anyone crossing over any lines of good taste, so keep your poems clean or I will have to bring your behaviour to the attention of Ms Whitehead for discipline upon her return.

Mrs. Carrell

Due: March 17

There will be no extensions given for this assignment. It is imperative that you use your class time effectively.

Assignment: My Limerick

By Arthur Bean

There once was a kid who's a nerd
He never liked following the herd
When a trend they would keep
He would "BAA" like a sheep
So they treated him just like a turd

Mr. Bean, the language and subject matter is clearly inappropriate, despite clear instructions in the assignment. See me after class.

Mrs. Carrell

▶▶ ▶▶ ▶▶

143

Ms Whitehead has asked me to start the next unit on Famous Authors. We'll be studying the lives of some of the great poets and novelists of yore. I would like each of you to write two to four paragraphs about your favourite author. Please talk about his or her life and career. Are you inspired by their life story or something they wrote? Why is he/she your favourite author? Do you have a favourite book by them? Make sure your grammar and spelling are correct and that you use different types of sentences.

Due: March 24

There will be no extensions given on this assignment.

March 18th

Dear RJ,

I tried starting my snake trainer story, but I can't get anywhere. I have nothing to say about it. All I got was a description of the fog, and it was so boring, I almost put myself to sleep. Plus I couldn't come up with an actual plot. All I have is a snake trainer and snakes that can be trained to commit crimes. It's not enough. I don't even like it anymore. Back to the drawing board. Watching TV is helpful, right? Because that's all I feel like doing.

Yours truly,
Arthur Bean

▶▶ ▶▶ ▶▶

From: Kennedy Laurel (imsocutekl@hotmail.com)
To: Arthur Bean (arthuraaronbean@gmail.com)
Sent: March 19, 14:55

Hi Arthur!

I've finally finished my story!! At least, I think it's
done! It's pretty different now than the first part I
sent to you LOL! But I really like it! I'm sure you're
CRAZY busy right now, but if you have time, can you
read it before I submit it? I think you'll give me good
feedback on it, and that you'll be honest if there's
anything I need to change!

I gave it to my parents, but they just said that it was
awesome LOL! Parents!! Sometimes they are really
nice, but they aren't very helpful LOL! Anyway, it's
pretty long, so if you're too busy to read it, that's ok
too! I know you're busy getting your story ready too!!

Kennedy ☺

From: Arthur Bean (arthuraaronbean@gmail.com)
To: Kennedy Laurel (imsocutekl@hotmail.com)
Sent: March 19, 15:13

Dear Kennedy,

I would love to read your story! I am pretty busy
putting the finishing touches on my story too, but I'm
never too busy for you. My mom used to say that I
have an eagle eye for detail, so I can give you good
feedback for sure.

I know what you mean about feedback from
parents. My dad sometimes reads what I write and

then he tells me that it should be published. My mom was good for finding mistakes, but sometimes she was crazy about finding mistakes in my grammar. I mean, who even knows what a participle is? Who cares?

Yours truly,
Arthur Bean

From: Kennedy Laurel (imsocutekl@hotmail.com)
To: Arthur Bean (arthuraaronbean@gmail.com)
Sent: March 19, 20:34

LOL! I had to go look up what a participle was to know what you were talking about!
   Thanks Arthur! That's so sweet of you to take time to do this for me! I've attached it here.

Kennedy ☺

Attachment included: **Strangers Among Us**

STRANGERS AMONG US

The brains of the alien were lavender and slate, and splattered all over Sophie's perfectly matched brown and pink off-the-shoulder top and dark skinny jeans. She flicked her ponytail over her shoulder, showing off her rosebud earrings.
   "Well? What should we do with it now?" she asked, slinging her bazooka over her left shoulder. She wiped the crimson blood from her hands on her back pockets, and looked over.

"I'd say we should bury it. Real deep," Tom replied. He looked at his own navy coveralls, covered with a red and green flannel shirt and also splattered with the rest of the alien's insides.

"Well, I guess we should start digging," Sophie said, reaching for the shovel . . .

Sophie woke with a start. She'd had that dream again. She sat up and shivered. The dreams were getting worse. Dreams, though? No. She knew they were more than that. The aliens were real. She had seen them. She had strangled one until its eyeballs burst out of its head. There was a gargantuan mess of crimson and white and light blue tendons all over her favourite teal dress, the one with the black piping and oversized buttons at the collar. She couldn't make that up. She had the dry cleaning bill to prove it. She shut her eyes and wished for the morning to come.

Sophie woke up early the next morning with a plan. She knew that her Uncle Tom had a barn full of weapons to fight with. She just had to get there before the aliens did.

She looked around for the fastest way to get out of town and spotted her favourite car, a bright red Corvette convertible. She ran over to it and looked inside. Luckily, the keys were still sitting in the ignition.

"Well, I don't have time to stand around looking pretty," said Sophie, tossing her long chestnut ponytail to the side and adjusting her favourite purple hoodie. "There's a war to fight!"

Sophie got in behind the wheel and the convertible roared to life. She threw it into drive and pulled out, heading down the highway to her uncle's farm.

Sophie hoped that Uncle Tom still had the bazooka in the barn, next to the cows. As a kid, Tom had told her stories of aliens her whole life. She knew the aliens had tried to take over the world and failed three times before, but each time they left a few aliens behind. Spies, Tom called them. They were hiding in disguises that made them look like very ugly humans, and the aliens ran dollar stores and late-night pizza windows. If they were launching their full attack now, Sophie was sure she wouldn't be eating pizza for a while.

She quickly reached Tom's farm. "Oh no!" The house and the barn were on fire. Sophie ran over to the farmhouse, calling Tom's name through her tears. He had to still be alive! He just *had* to!

Just then she heard a muffled cry from the barn. She listened again and heard her name carried on the wind. "Uncle Tom!" she cried, and ran into the smoking barn, where she found Tom in a corner under some hay. He was hurt, badly, but he was alive!

"They've taken almost everything," Tom said. "They're here, and they're going to take over! You've got to stop them!"

"But how can I do that?" said Sophie.

"Build a bomb. They were heading to the hospital next. They are evil and sneaky aliens. Bomb the hospital and you can take them out," Tom said. "You must get all the fertilizer from the farm. You can build an explosive big enough to take them all out." Tom closed his eyes and went limp.

"Tom! No!" Sophie sobbed. Sophie cried for a while, then wiped her eyes and stood up. "Now I must save the world. For Uncle Tom. For me," she said to herself. "Quick Sophie. Get to work!"

Sophie worked hard to gather all the fertilizer, and some gasoline and matches. She loaded it all into Tom's pickup truck and drove back into town in silence. She arrived at the hospital. It was eerily quiet.

"The aliens must be here," said Sophie. "I'd better make the fertilizer bomb." She decided to put piles of fertilizer at the four corners of the hospital, watching out for any aliens or people. Her thoughts turned to her old friends, now dead because of alien attacks, and she shivered. That could have been Sophie. But instead of thinking about it too much, she continued working, and soon she had four large piles of fertilizer and put them on the hospital corners.

Just then she heard a noise. It was a growling noise, and it was getting louder and louder. Sophie looked around, but she didn't see anything. Then the noise was high-pitched, and soon she couldn't hear anything except the screeching. It sounded like a thousand nails on a chalkboard. Finally Sophie looked up. Hovering above her was a giant round disc. It was the alien ship! It was so close that she could see alien heads in the windows. Their tiny mouths were open, like they were talking, but all Sophie could hear was the screeching.

Suddenly, she felt something whoosh past her, and she jumped into the car. Something exploded! She screamed, but her voice was drowned out by the horrible noises of the aliens. "No! I won't let you do this to my world!" Sophie cried, and ran to the stack of gasoline cans in the field. She pulled the pack of matches out of her pocket. The alien ship was descending closer to her, and when she looked up she was able to see their tiny nostrils twitching like a bunny nose.

Sophie watched with horror through the window as an alien lowered itself into a girl's body and then zipped it up again, like the human body was a jacket. The girl-alien stood up and twitched her nose, then stared down at Sophie. Sophie was propelled into action. She tried four more matches before one of them caught fire, and she threw it down onto the gas cans. Suddenly there was a blast of fire and the ship moved higher into the sky like a giant hand pushed it up. Sophie squatted down close to the ground and watched the fire snake across the field towards the hospital. The flash was blinding when the fire hit the first fertilizer pile, and she kneeled down with her arms over her head. The sound was deafening, and Sophie felt the heat as each pile exploded. She looked up, only to see a giant piece of concrete heading right for her. "NOOOO!" she screamed, but there was nowhere to go. The world went black.

Sophie woke up and was lying in a hospital bed, with a giant bandage covering most of her head. She tried to sit up, but found that her arms were restrained to the rails on the bed. A nurse came into the room.

"Oh! You're awake! That's great!" the nurse said in a chipper voice.

"What happened?" Sophie asked groggily.

"Well, there was a fertilizer explosion at your uncle's farm. You got hit with concrete. You almost died. Thankfully, we are here to take care of you," the nurse said. Then her eyes narrowed. "You are lucky we are here. We are here to take care of everyone on Earth. Forever," the nurse said. She twitched her nose. Sophie stared at her, and she was certain she could hear the sound of someone's nails on a chalkboard coming from down the hall.

The End

March 19th

Dear RJ,

It's official.

I'm totally screwed.

▶▶ ▶▶ ▶▶

JUNIOR AUTHORS CONTEST

This is a reminder that your stories are due on April 1st
at the end of the day. One more week to put your final
touches on your story! Good luck to everyone entering
the contest; it's been a pleasure working with all of
you and seeing the creative juices flowing.
Choosing the finalists will certainly be difficult!

March 20th

Dear RJ,

OK, RJ. I'm not kidding this time. We've got to
come up with a story. I had one last night in
my dreams, but I've forgotten it now. It's not
fair!

I wish I had electrodes on my brain that
were connected to a computer that was writing
everything down. I should invent that. Then
I could be a famous inventor, because at this
rate, I'm sure not going to be a famous writer!

Anyway, RJ, I need help. I can't lose this
competition. It's just not an option. I'll do

151

anything for a story idea right now. I tried calling Luke too, but he's away for a hockey tournament this weekend, so I can't even talk to him. What am I going to do?

Yours truly,
Arthur Bean

▶▶ ▶▶ ▶▶

From: Kennedy Laurel (imsocutekl@hotmail.com)
To: Arthur Bean (arthuraaronbean@gmail.com)
Sent: March 21, 19:08

Hi Arthur! Have you had a chance to read my story yet?? I never heard back from you! Maybe you think it's terrible, and don't know how to tell me ☹
   Do you think it's OK? Did the ending make sense? I tried to get your attention during lunch today, but you didn't see me, I guess!
   There's a rehearsal tomorrow at lunch, so maybe you can give me your feedback then! I would really <u>really</u> appreciate it! Normally you're so good at getting back to me really fast! You've got me worried!

Kennedy ☺

▶▶ ▶▶ ▶▶

From: Kennedy Laurel (imsocutekl@hotmail.com)
To: Arthur Bean (arthuraaronbean@gmail.com)
Sent: March 22, 16:23

Hi Arthur!

Mr. Tan said that you said you had extra work to do
in Math today, and couldn't make rehearsal! I missed
you! We ended up working on the scene I have with
Ben instead! He's going to be an AWESOME nurse . . .
so funny! I was looking forward to talking to you about
my story! You must be pretty busy finishing your story!
I haven't heard from you at all! Maybe we can hang out
before rehearsal and you can give me some feedback!
I would really like that! Hopefully see you tomorrow!

Kennedy ☺

From: Kennedy Laurel (imsocutekl@hotmail.com)
To: Arthur Bean (arthuraaronbean@gmail.com)
Sent: March 22, 23:44

Hi Arthur! I'm starting to think you're avoiding me!
PLEASE PLEASE can you send me even a short
email saying that my story is OK! I've been reading
it over and over to see if there's something I should
change, but I don't know what that would be! Is it
full of spelling mistakes? Does it suck?? I'm going
CRAZY over here! I just want it to be good enough
to not be embarrassing!

Kennedy ☺

▶▶　▶▶　▶▶

Artie read the draft of my author piece and
said it was good. he fixed alot of misstakes and
showed me where I used anyway alot. he fixed
it and now its better.
— Robbie

Robbie's essay on Chris Van Allsburg was
interesting. I didn't know you could illustrate
an essay. I wish more essays were illustrated. I
didn't know anything about the guy at all, and
now I learned something. That Chris guy is a
pretty good illustrator, and I like that Robbie
added some of his pictures into his essay. I never
really read any of his stuff, but Robbie was
showing me some really cool books that are cool
even though they are picture books for kids. I
don't know if they really are for kids.

   Robbie's paragraph about magic in books was
interesting too.
— Arthur

➤➤ ➤➤ ➤➤

My Favourite Author

By Arthur Bean

Arthur Bean was born in a hospital in Winnipeg,
Manitoba. His parents, Ernest and Margaret
Bean, were ecstatic and proclaimed his talents
early. Moving to Calgary when Arthur was only

two years old, Arthur quickly became a fixture in the literary scene. He was reading chapter books before his seventh birthday, and decided to be an author quickly thereafter. His first poem, called "Rain," was published in the school newsletter in grade five, setting his career into motion.

After "Rain," Arthur's stories took on a more serious tone. The playful nature of his first poem was subtly mocked in his first short story called "Lightning Storms over Disneyland." He began developing his characters in more realistic ways in his story "Sockland," a break-through story that got highly positive reviews from Mrs. Lewis, a highly regarded grade six teacher.

Arthur's writing career was put on hiatus after Marg Bean died last year. She was his muse and greatest fan. But he has come back full force with a strong manuscript in the city-wide writing competition. He expects to win $200, his first prize in what promises to be a long writing career. He is also an amateur actor and investigative journalist.

Arthur's career means a lot to me because it is mine. I think he captures what I am feeling and thinking in what he writes, and he is very clever.

Mr. Bean,

This is an unacceptable interpretation of this assignment. This kind of snide mocking of the assignment is juvenile, unoriginal and rude. I expect you to take home this letter to your parents and return it with a signature tomorrow.

Mrs. Carrell

March 24th

Dear RJ,

Mrs. Carrell is ruining my life. How am I
supposed to write a story when she is clearly
trying to make me lose the competition? She
knows that the deadline is a week away, and
she still gives us homework. Plus she sucks
any fun out of writing too. She keeps yelling
at me, and when she's not yelling, she has
this look on her face like she is about to yell
at me. She even yells at me when I haven't
done anything! Like today, my pencil broke
and I needed to sharpen it, and when I went to
empty the pencil sharpener into the garbage,
she said that I was disrupting the class! I was
just emptying the pencil sharpener, and then
she sent me into the hall! What did I ever do to
her?

Yours truly,
Arthur Bean

From: Arthur Bean (arthuraaronbean@gmail.com)
To: Kennedy Laurel (imsocutekl@hotmail.com)
Sent: March 24, 21:09

Dear Kennedy,

I'm really sorry I didn't get back to you earlier. I didn't
get a chance to read your story. I was hoping to find
time to read it, but I've been really busy. I'm sure that
your story is awesome! I think you are probably my

fiercest competition! And there's spell-check on the computer to catch any spelling mistakes, so I don't think you need to worry there.

Anyway, I should get back to writing my own story, but good luck with your final draft! I'm sure it's perfect!

Yours truly,
Arthur Bean

From: Kennedy Laurel (imsocutekl@hotmail.com)
To: Arthur Bean (arthuraaronbean@gmail.com)
Sent: March 24, 21:19

Thanks Arthur!

Of course you didn't have a chance to read it! You're like the busiest person in the world! I should've thought about that more, especially knowing that you're in the play, and writing for the newspaper, AND writing a novel, AND writing your own story for the competition! It's crazy! Can you imagine what it will be like when we're adults with JOBS LOL! Anyway, I'm so RELIEVED to get your email! And you said such nice things! You are TOO sweet!

Kennedy ☺

March 27th

Dear RJ,

Stories are due soon, and I've written nothing!
Not even a word.

Why did I ever think I could be a writer?
I have all these ideas in my head, but I don't
know how to write them down. Or else I tell
Nicole or Luke about them, and then when I
try to write them down, all my ideas are gone.
It's like someone took them away as soon as
I said them out loud. I can't make my brain
work. I can't even make my fingers type. Or if I
get an idea that I don't talk about, I don't know
where to start. Then I think about the ideas,
and they're stupid. All of them are stupid. I'm
stupid. I'm never going to be famous. Ever.
Where can I get a story in three days?

Yours truly,
Arthur Bean

▸▸ ▸▸ ▸▸

Peer Tutoring Program — Progress Report
Session: March 29th
Worked On: Short Story

Robbie's story was good, except for the mistakes
and stuff.
— Arthur

Artie helpd me with my camp storey, cuz I finnished it erly.
— Robbie

Gentlemen:

I understand that you are working together on a weekly basis, but in my books, this is an unacceptable synopsis of your work. I am certain this would not fly with Ms Whitehead and it certainly does not fly with me. In the future, I expect to see something concrete that you have worked on together.

Mrs. Carrell

▶▶ ▶▶ ▶▶

From: Arthur Bean (arthuraaronbean@gmail.com)
To: Robbie Zack (robbiethegreat2000@hotmail.com)
Sent: March 30, 02:04

Dear Robbie,

I know you don't owe me any favours at all, but I have
a big one to ask of you. I need to use the short story
that you showed me the other day. I think it's really
good.

There's a long explanation, but I don't have
anything to put in for the writing competition. It's
hard to explain. I don't have a story, and I need one,
and you have good ideas and the ghost story you
wrote would be perfect. I'll give you anything you
want. I can pay you for it. I just really need it, and I will
be grateful if I could have it.

Yours truly,
Arthur Bean

From: Robbie Zack (robbiethegreat2000@hotmail.com)
To: Arthur Bean (arthuraaronbean@gmail.com)
Sent: March 30, 08:22

I dont get it. why do u need my storey? why should i
give it to u anyway? i dont want ur money. tell me why
u need it, and ill decide from there.

From: Arthur Bean (arthuraaronbean@gmail.com)
To: Robbie Zack (robbiethegreat2000@hotmail.com)
Sent: March 30, 08:43

Dear Robbie,

I need your story because I promised my dad I
would win the competition because he's sad about
my mom dying, and my grandma told me that she
would die of a heart attack if I didn't win, and I bet
my next door neighbour Nicole $5 that I would win,
and it's really important to them that I win because
otherwise I will be a failure and let down my whole
family because I'm supposed to be a famous author
and I can't be a famous author without winning a
competition.

   Please don't tell anyone. I need to put a story in
tomorrow and I need your help.

Yours truly,
Arthur Bean

From: Robbie Zack (robbiethegreat2000@hotmail.com)
To: Arthur Bean (arthuraaronbean@gmail.com)
Sent: March 30, 12:08

That's alot of reasons artie. i also think, u owe me
something big. heres the deal: u tell mr. Tan that u r
dropping out of the play and i get to be romeo and i
will give u my storey

From: Arthur Bean (arthuraaronbean@gmail.com)
To: Robbie Zack (robbiethegreat2000@hotmail.com)
Sent: March 30, 12:22

Dear Robbie,

I don't think that's a very good trade. I have a lot
of money. I can pay you as much as you want, but
I really, <u>really</u> want to be in the play.
How about $50?
I can give you $50 for your story.

Yours truly,
Arthur Bean

From: Robbie Zack (robbiethegreat2000@hotmail.com)
To: Arthur Bean (arthuraaronbean@gmail.com)
Sent: March 30, 15:44

i dont want your $. romeo for storey.

From: Arthur Bean (arthuraaronbean@gmail.com)
To: Robbie Zack (robbiethegreat2000@hotmail.com)
Sent: March 30, 16:19

Dear Robbie,

What about $100? I would have to give it to you in
two parts though, but I can get the money.
I don't think you want to be Romeo anyway. There
are so many lines to memorize, and Mr. Tan is really
strict in rehearsals.

Also, the reflections are a total pain to write, and the rehearsals can be really long and boring. I'm sure you have better stuff to do.

Yours truly,
Arthur Bean

From: Arthur Bean (arthuraaronbean@gmail.com)
To: Robbie Zack (robbiethegreat2000@hotmail.com)
Sent: March 30, 19:05

Dear Robbie,

Do you want more money? I could give you the prize money! I kind of wanted it to get my dad something, but I can give you that if you want. Please don't make me give up the part!

Yours truly,
Arthur Bean

From: Arthur Bean (arthuraaronbean@gmail.com)
To: Robbie Zack (robbiethegreat2000@hotmail.com)
Sent: March 30, 20:00

Dear Robbie,

Fine. You can be Romeo. Can you send me your story tonight? I think that it's really good, but I'm going to make it even better, and I'm sure there are spelling mistakes I'll need to fix.

Arthur

From: Robbie Zack (robbiethegreat2000@hotmail.com)
To: Arthur Bean (arthuraaronbean@gmail.com)
Sent: March 30, 20:03

THANKS ARTIE! Heres my storey for you. im really glad to be playing romeo i think i will do a good job. anyway i am taller than kennedy so i think we will look good onstage next to each other more than you guys did. this makes my year. anyway i thought this year would suck!

Attachment included: **Ghost Love Storey**

APRIL

Arthur Bean
Ms Whitehead
Class 7A

GHOST LOVE STORY

Before he died, Jack sat behind Kaylee in Math class.
Instead of learning about fractions, he studied her
back. Her brown hair covered her neck. She rarely
put her hair in a ponytail. Sometimes the tag of her
shirt stuck out. She wore a medium.

Jack was average. He didn't do very well in Math,
and he hated English. He was pretty good at Gym,
and he liked Art. He had a few friends, but he could
have used more.

When school ended, summer vacation began. The
only reason Jack cared about summer vacation was
the fact that he wasn't going to see Kaylee for two
months. Seeing Kaylee every day in Math class made
Jack so happy.

During summer vacation Jack went to camp. Jack
liked camp. It was at a lake and the kids were nice
and they drew pictures of nature and did rubbings
on rocks and acted out funny skits at night. They
got to learn to sail and swim in the lake and play
capture the flag. It was like Gym and Art class put
together.

It was Saturday when it started raining at camp.
One rain day is OK because the camp had some
movies to watch in the big lodge. But then it

rained on Sunday. Monday, Tuesday, Wednesday, Thursday. All rain. By Friday everyone was so sick of the lodge that when Jack suggested a rainy swim in the lake, lots of kids agreed. The counsellors were tired of coming up with indoor activities, so they agreed too. They played Rock Paper Scissors to see who had to stand watch out in the rain. Brooke lost.

The lake seemed really warm compared to the cold rain. Jack preferred to stay under the water for as long as he could. When he couldn't hold his breath any longer, he would burst through the surface for a big gasp of air. Jack dove under over and over. He would grab the younger kids by their ankles and listen for them to shriek and kick him away. He did this for hours until he was the only kid left swimming. Brooke was cold and wet and grumpy.

"Jack! Are you going to be in there all day?" she called out.

Jack nodded.

"You OK if I go inside?" she asked.

Jack nodded again. Then he dove under the water, into the warmth of the reeds. When he surfaced, he was alone. He smiled and swam out a little farther, then ducked under the water.

He never came back up.

It was a few hours before anyone noticed that Jack hadn't come in from the lake. They looked for him, but Jack knew they wouldn't find him. No one was going to look for him tangled in the reeds at the bottom of the lake. He was just a ghost, floating above them now. The counsellors called the police. They brought their search and rescue boat. Jack was pleased that he was so important, and he hovered over the bow of the boat when they went out into the middle of the lake.

The police were grumpy in the rain. They called him a "stupid kid" for swimming out so far. He tried to punch them in the face, but his fist never hit anything. They found his body in the reeds. The police pretended to be sad when they pulled up to the dock.

When school started again, nobody seemed to miss Jack. This made him sad. He wanted people to wear black arm bands and maybe put a large photo of him in the trophy case, like schools in movies do for students who have died. But no one did anything. He thought maybe his favourite teacher would leave his desk in homeroom empty, as a tribute. Instead, everyone moved up a desk to replace him. He thought that maybe there would be a moment of silence for him at the beginning of Art class, but his teacher just started teaching pastel techniques.

The worst was Kaylee. Kaylee didn't notice at all. She didn't cry or even ask anyone about him. It was like he had never been alive in the first place. It sucked.

Jack sat on the desk behind hers and stared at her back. She still wore a medium. Her hair was longer. She stared at Olivier, the French exchange student, and purred *"Bonjour"* at him when he looked at her. Jack thought that was really annoying. But other than that, she was still nice.

Still, she didn't notice he was gone.

So Jack decided to make her notice. He followed her home and watched TV sitting next to her on the couch. He curled up beside her on her bed when she was reading. He went to every volleyball game, every play rehearsal, every swimming lesson.

Then Kaylee started feeling cold at night. She smiled less. She seemed . . . sad, somehow. She had never seemed sad before.

Jack worried about her. *Maybe she's sad about me,* he thought to himself. *Maybe she's realizing that I'm gone.*

Jack was getting stronger as a ghost. He found that he could move the curtains, just a whisper. He would rush back and forth through the curtains, and they would flicker. Each time he would blow the curtains in Kaylee's living room, she would look up. He smiled to himself. She was starting to notice him. So he made a plan to make her notice more.

One night, Kaylee's parents went out to bowling, leaving her alone. The rain started around six, and by seven there was a huge lightning storm. The storm fuelled Jack's ghost powers, making him super-strong.

Jack started off small. He swooshed the curtains around. He rattled the glasses. Kaylee shivered when he moved around her. He slammed the bathroom door. He jiggled the doorknobs. He pushed her pens so they would roll off the table.

"Ghost?" she called out to Jack. "I know you're here!" she cried. But the only answer was the sound of her pencil clattering to the floor. "Go away!" she yelled into the air.

"It's so cold," she whispered to herself as Jack moved back and forth, causing her teeth to chatter. Finally she stood up and went upstairs to get a sweater. She grabbed a hoodie off her floor and struggled to pull it on.

Jack took hold of one of the sleeves and pulled as hard as he could. The sleeve twisted around to the back. Kaylee had her head in the sweater and was pulling on the sleeve, trying to unwind it from the back. She walked towards the stairs. Just then there was an earth-shattering crash of lightning.

Kaylee was caught off guard and she tripped. Jack watched helplessly as she tumbled headfirst down the stairs. She lay still at the bottom. Her hoodie still covered her face. Her neck was at a funny angle.

Jack yelled, but there was no sound. He cried, but no one heard him. Finally he curled up next to Kaylee and cried. He tried to hold her hand. "I love you," he wept. "I really, really love you."

Then he felt something cold and clammy tighten around his fingers.

Kaylee's ghost blinked at him. Then she smiled. "Are you a ghost?" she said. Jack nodded.

She sat up and looked down at herself.

"Am I a ghost?"

Jack nodded.

"Will you show me around, Ghost?" She smiled at him and flipped her ghost hair.

Jack nodded.

"You're cute, Ghost. What's your name?" she said.

"Jack," Jack whispered.

"Jack," she said. "Did I know you before?"

Jack nodded. "I've loved you forever."

Kaylee smiled shyly. "I guess I better catch up then." She kissed his cheek. "Now, can you show me how you do that curtain thing?"

And they died happily ever after.

The End

Hiya, Arthur!

Your story looks great. I'll add it the to pile of finalists. I'm going to be working on the Science Fair (and, hey! I didn't get your proposal . . .) and track and field tryouts are this week, so I might not get to read everything before printing — there are a few "hurdles" for this new track coach!

The newspaper will be out just before spring break, and voting will start after we get back, so watch for the ballot. I'm sure you will want to cast a vote for yourself; you can get a leg up on the competition!

Speaking of spring break, the Spring Fling Dance is coming up. It's a Sadie Hawkins theme, which means that the girls ask the boys! Very old-fashioned thinking, in my opinion, but I'm not leading the social committee, am I?

Would you be able to cover the dance for the newspaper?

Let me know!

Cheers,
Mr. E.

Dear Mr. Everett,

I was thinking that I could write my own article for the next edition. I was thinking it could be like "An Insider's View on the Competition." It would be about winning the writing competition and

stuff. I'm pretty sure that I will win,
and I'm sure that other students would
be interested in what that is like.

Yours truly,
Arthur Bean

Hiya, A,

I'm glad you're so confident, but let's not
count our chickens before they hatch! I
think I hear some clucking coming from
you! Plus, we really need a piece on the
dance after spring break. Are you ready
to bust a move?

Cheers,
Mr. E.

▶▶ ▶▶ ▶▶

Romeo and Juliet — a Star's Reflection

By Romeo

Act 2, Scene 4
In this scene I am planning something with the
enemy. Well, not really the enemy anymore, but
Juliet's nurse. We have to be devious to get away
with what I am planning, so we make secret
plans that no one knows about. I feel good and
bad about it. I am glad that I am getting what I
want (marrying and kissing Juliet), but I have
to give up something as well (my family). I feel

very torn about it. It is like a time when I was seven and my cousin Luke wanted to switch Christmas presents with me. I really, really liked my present, but I really, really wanted his present too. But I couldn't have both, so I chose his present over mine. I still think about that Christmas. I don't know if I should have switched. I miss my real present, even though it was only mine for a day or two.

Arthur, you've tapped into a strong memory to work from, and I think this will translate nicely into your acting. This week we're heading into some of the scenes with some heavy feelings. Keep digging into your memories and building your character!

Mr. Tan

▶▶ ▶▶ ▶▶

From: Robbie Zack (robbiethegreat2000@hotmail.com)
To: Arthur Bean (arthuraaronbean@gmail.com)
Sent: April 4, 15:54

i saw u in the drama room today practising R&J. u r NOT in the play anymore anyway.
    u better tell mr Tan tomorrow or i will tell some one about "ur" storey

robbie

From: Arthur Bean (arthuraaronbean@gmail.com)
To: Robbie Zack (robbiethegreat2000@hotmail.com)
Sent: April 4, 20:14

Dear Robbie,

You hadn't brought up the play in a few days, so I
thought maybe you had decided that you didn't want
to be in it. I figured that you would have thought
about that over the weekend and realized how much
work it is.

But I will tell Mr. Tan this week.

You do know there are rehearsals through spring
break, right? If you are going away for the week, you
can't be in the play.

Are you going to visit your mom? I bet she misses
you.

Yours truly,
Arthur Bean

From: Robbie Zack (robbiethegreat2000@hotmail.com)
To: Arthur Bean (arthuraaronbean@gmail.com)
Sent: April 4, 21:13

dont make me come after you

r

From: Arthur Bean (arthuraaronbean@gmail.com)
To: Robbie Zack (robbiethegreat2000@hotmail.com)
Sent: April 4, 20:14

Dear Robbie,

No need for you to join me. I will talk to Mr. Tan
tomorrow, I guess.

Yours truly,
Arthur Bean

▶▶ ▶▶ ▶▶

Dear Mr. Tan,

I've realized that I can't participate in
the play anymore. My duties as a student
are more important, and I need to
focus on my writing.

Acting is really a secondary skill for me,
and since I want to be a writer and
not an actor, I am hereby dropping
out of the school play. Robbie Zack, my
understudy, has agreed to take my part
as Romeo very seriously.

Yours truly,
Arthur Bean

Dear Arthur,

PLEASE come and see me anytime today. I would like to discuss your decision with you. This is not something I take lightly.

Mr. Tan

From: Kennedy Laurel (imsocutekl@hotmail.com)
To: Arthur Bean (arthuraaronbean@gmail.com)
Sent: April 5, 19:39

ARTHUR!! What is up?!?!?! Mr. Tan told us today in rehearsal that you QUIT the play?!?! I thought you LOVED being in the play!! We missed you today! I mean, Robbie is really nice but we have to start rehearsing scenes ALL OVER AGAIN! What happened? Why aren't you in the play anymore? I totally don't understand!

Kennedy ☹

April 5th

Dear RJ,

I hate myself! I can't believe I am stupid enough to give up my ONE chance to make Kennedy fall in love with me just so that I can be famous! Does every famous person have to make difficult decisions like this? What if she falls in love with Robbie and then they get married? I'll be famous and alone, and people will always look at me with pity in their eyes. It will be worse than when Mom died because they will look at me like that FOREVER. I'll go on talk shows to promote my book and I'll have to joke about "the one that got away" . . . but it won't be a joke!

Now it's spring break and we're not even going to visit Luke's family. I'll just be at home or sitting at Nicole's house, thinking about how I will be alone forever.

Yours truly,
Arthur Bean

From: Arthur Bean (arthuraaronbean@gmail.com)
To: Kennedy Laurel (imsocutekl@hotmail.com)
Sent: April 5, 23:03

Dear Kennedy,

I'm sorry to quit the play like that. I did what I had to do for my art. You know, my novel and such. I really didn't want to, but I had to do it.

It's too bad you're away for spring break. At least, I think you are. I accidentally overheard you telling Catie you were going away. I hope you have fun!

Yours truly,
Arthur Bean

▶▶   ▶▶   ▶▶

April 12th

Dear RJ,

This is officially the worst spring break ever.
There's nowhere to go and nothing to do. My dad
only took a couple of days off, but even then, we
just went to my grandparents' house. It snowed
the whole time, and my grandma just wanted to
go to the drugstore. I wish she would make a list
of stuff she needed so that we didn't have to go
every day.

When we got home yesterday, Dad told me
that he thought I was responsible enough to
stay at home alone on the days when Nicole
is at work. I thought it would be cool, but it's
really not. Daytime TV sucks, and Pickles wasn't
used to having someone around, so she just
kept clawing my hand every time I tried to get
the remote from under her. I got so bored that
I did all my homework, and I even tried writing
my short story for Ms Whitehead's class. I
didn't get very far. I thought maybe working on
Robbie's story would get my brain going again,
but I'm still sitting here with the computer on,
staring at a blank screen. I wish there was
something, ANYTHING to do. I'm desperate, RJ.
I'm debating buying a bus ticket and going to
see Luke. I won't, because I don't want my dad
to think I ran away, but still. It's SO BORING!

Yours truly,
Arthur Bean

▶▶ ▶▶ ▶▶

From: Robbie Zack (robbiethegreat2000@hotmail.com)
To: Arthur Bean (arthuraaronbean@gmail.com)
Sent: April 13, 11:04

hey artie

i heard u r in town for the break. no 1 else is. anyway i
won these tickets to a play and none of my real frends
wood want 2 come with me. i bearly want to go but i
figur its good 2 see other plays now that im staring in
1. anyway, did u want 2 come 2 a play with my brother
and me. my dad was gonna come but he cant and
now we have a spare ticket and i bet u like plays and
stuf. the play is on tomorro nite so let me kno. And
can ur dad drive us?

Robbie

From: Arthur Bean (arthuraaronbean@gmail.com)
To: Robbie Zack (robbiethegreat2000@hotmail.com)
Sent: April 13, 12:29

Are you serious?

From: Robbie Zack (robbiethegreat2000@hotmail.com)
To: Arthur Bean (arthuraaronbean@gmail.com)
Sent: April 13, 12:36

No nerd i am writing u for fun. OF COURSE im
serious. do u want to come or not. i don't care either
way.

From: Arthur Bean (arthuraaronbean@gmail.com)
To: Robbie Zack (robbiethegreat2000@hotmail.com)
Sent: April 13, 14:15

Dear Robbie,

I can go to the play I guess. I asked my dad and he
can drive us. We can pick you guys up at 7:00. See
you then.

Yours truly,
Arthur Bean

▶▶ ▶▶ ▶▶

April 14th

Dear RJ,

Weirdest night ever! I went to a play with Robbie
and his brother. I know what you're thinking —
and, I know, it WAS weird. Robbie's brother is a
total jerk. Robbie actually even apologized to me
because his brother was so strange. I thought
Robbie was bad and annoying sometimes, but
his brother was yelling at people in the lobby
and laughing, and he kept trying to get people
to spill their drinks by bumping into them in the
lobby. It was super embarrassing. I was glad to
get into the play.

   It was pretty good. I thought it was going
to be a little kids' play when he told me
we were going to see *Peter Pan*, but it was
actually pretty cool and professional. The
actors were awesome, but I think I would
have been better as Peter Pan. I liked the way

the actors flew on harnesses, and I thought
Tinkerbell was pretty hot. And Robbie totally
loved the play. I think he even cried at the
end. But I'm sure he was wiping his eyes
when Wendy and the boys came home. His
brother saw him crying too, and made fun of
him the whole way home.

Anyway, when they got out Robbie asked
me if I wanted to come over and play video
games this weekend. I kind of hate video
games, especially if you have to shoot things.
I think they are super boring. But I said yes
anyway. I don't know why he asked me. I kind
of had to say yes. I mean, would he beat me up
if I said no?

Yours truly,
Arthur Bean

▶▶ ▶▶ ▶▶

April 17th

Dear RJ,

Happy Easter! The week is almost over! Finally!
And my dad is cooking a ham tonight, with
scalloped potatoes. I didn't even know he
knew how to do that. I don't know what came
over him. He even put out chocolate eggs for
an Easter egg hunt for me this morning. I
was so surprised, especially since I haven't
done an Easter egg hunt for, like, five years or
something. I didn't say that though. He said
that he always hid the eggs, and this year he

made it really hard. It's funny. I guess I always thought my mom did that kind of stuff. I guess it makes sense why she was always so surprised to see where the eggs were. I just thought she was a good actress.

So I did the Easter egg hunt, and then we went for a walk to the farmers' market to get stuff for supper. It was pretty quiet while we walked, but it was quiet in a good way this time. He even asked if I wanted to invite my "new friend Robbie" for supper. I told him that Robbie was definitely not my friend, he was just bored over spring break and needed another person to compete against in his video game (which I hated, by the way. I suck a lot at video games, RJ. Robbie made sure to tell me that a lot).

Anyway, it's been a pretty good day, RJ. I don't know why, but I even sort of felt for a minute that Mom was just away somewhere, like she was visiting her sister or something. I almost feel bad for feeling good about Easter. That's weird, isn't it?

Yours truly,
Arthur Bean

▶▶ ▶▶ ▶▶

From: Kennedy Laurel (imsocutekl@hotmail.com)
To: Arthur Bean (arthuraaronbean@gmail.com)
Sent: April 19, 15:50

Hi Arthur!

Sorry I didn't respond about spring break! I went to
visit my grandma and she has NO INTERNET! It was
TORTURE LOL!! Well, it was OK but kind of boring!
My little sister was SUPER annoying too and wanted
me to HANG OUT with her! So frustrating! It's way
better when there's something to keep her busy like
the computer LOL! At least I had lots of time to learn
all my lines for the play!

   Speaking of the play, I can't believe you aren't in it
anymore! I went to rehearsal today and you weren't
there and it wasn't as fun! You always make me laugh
when I see you! I mean Robbie tries really hard and
he's super sweet, but it's just different, you know?
Anyway, I guess you're really busy writing and stuff!

Kennedy ☺

From: Arthur Bean (arthuraaronbean@gmail.com)
To: Kennedy Laurel (imsocutekl@hotmail.com)
Sent: April 19, 18:22

Dear Kennedy,

I had a nice break. I had some time to work on my
writing. I also saw a good play with Robbie and his
brother, and went to a bunch of really cool parties.
It's too bad you weren't here to come to the parties.
They were really fun. It's too bad that I am no longer
in the play, but I told Mr. Tan that I will learn all the

lines just in case Robbie gets sick or too scared to go on stage. One of the reasons I stepped aside for the play was to give Robbie a chance to play Romeo. I know his mom left and I thought it would be good for him to have something good.

Yours truly,
Arthur Bean

From: Kennedy Laurel (imsocutekl@hotmail.com)
To: Arthur Bean (arthuraaronbean@gmail.com)
Sent: April 19, 19:23

Arthur that is so sweet! I knew there was something behind your motives to leave the play! I had no idea that you and Robbie were so close! That is just the nicest thing I've ever heard! We're both so lucky to have you as a friend Arthur!

Kennedy ☺

▸▸ ▸▸ ▸▸

Spring Has Sprung, Fling Is Fun

By Arthur Bean

Terry Fox Jr. High hosted its fourth dance of the year and finally got it right. The Spring Fling Dance held last Friday was a Sadie Hawkins Dance. Sadie Hawkins was originally a character in a comic strip from the 1930s. She was the ugliest girl in the town, and then her dad had a race in her name. If Sadie Hawkins caught a man and dragged him across the finish line, he had to marry her. The comic strip was pretty popular, and soon Sadie Hawkins races and dances were celebrated in Canada and the United States.

The highlight for most was definitely the opportunity to dance with some of the prettiest and most popular girls in school. For example, Kennedy Laurel's invitation to dance was met with enthusiastic yeses. Those of us lucky enough to be asked by such a graceful and energetic dancer as Kennedy were clearly watched with envy by the less fortunate of our gender.

There is one more dance this year for the entire school (not including the graduation class party held only for grade nines and their dates), and this reporter suggests that it also be a Sadie Hawkins Dance.

Hey, Arthur,

Nice work on covering the dance. I'm glad that you had fun at the same time!

I'm going to make a few changes to your work to be less specific about who danced with whom. I'm glad to see that you researched Sadie Hawkins too! Researching your subject is the key to great journalism, so well done!

Next up for you is a preview piece on the Spring Art Show. Most of the work will be up in the Art room in a couple of weeks.

Would you be able to do an article talking about the background of a few artists and their works? Remember though, just because a picture might be worth a thousand words doesn't mean your article needs to be too long!

Cheers,
Mr. E.

▶▶ ▶▶ ▶▶

JUNIOR AUTHORS CONTEST WINNERS!
We wish to thank all of you for your creativity, your
ideas and your fantastic writing. You made our jobs
very difficult to choose finalists for publication in
the spring edition of the *Marathon* newspaper!
Without further ado, the finalists are:
Arthur Bean
Asira Jaffer
Kennedy Laurel
Watch for a special Junior Authors edition of the *Marathon*
next week, and don't forget to VOTE for your favourite story!

From: Kennedy Laurel (imsocutekl@hotmail.com)
To: Arthur Bean (arthuraaronbean@gmail.com)
Sent: April 22, 16:39

Arthur! WE WON!!! I can't believe we're both
FINALISTS! This is AWESOME!! I'm so happy to
have gotten this far! And now I will win and get
published, and then I will take over the world LOL!!!
Just kidding! I'm so excited to be published in
the newspaper! I mean, it's different than being
published for writing just a boring old ARTICLE LOL!
   And CONGRATULATIONS to you! I never read this
masterful piece while you were writing it, and now I
will get to when it's published LOL! It's so exciting!
What is your story about?
   Doesn't it suck to be Ms Whitehead, stuck in bed
with a broken hip?! Are you going to send her a card
to thank her for choosing you? I think I will send one
to Mrs. Ireland!

Sandy is taking me out to a movie tonight to celebrate! What are YOU doing to celebrate? Something with your dad maybe? If you want to come with Sandy and I, you can totally tag along! I'm sure he won't mind!

Kennedy ☺

April 22nd

Dear RJ,

I made it! I was chosen as a finalist! AND, in even better news, Kennedy invited me to a movie tonight! She said that Sandy is going, but that's OK. Maybe she really just wants to go with me HAHAHA.

It's a joke now, RJ, but maybe a little bit serious? After all, we are both authors, and we can talk about writing and *Romeo and Juliet* and stuff. It could be that this is her subtle way to ask me on a date. It's so devious — right under her boyfriend's nose like that. But that's OK. I can hide stuff too.

Yours truly,
Arthur Bean

From: Arthur Bean (arthuraaronbean@gmail.com)
To: Kennedy Laurel (imsocutekl@hotmail.com)
Sent: April 22, 17:50

Dear Kennedy,

Thanks and congratulations to you also! I am not celebrating with my dad tonight, so I'd love to join you at the movies. Call me and let me know what movie you're going to, and I'll meet you there!

Yours truly,
Arthur Bean

April 22nd

Dear RJ,

Well that wasn't a date AT ALL. I went to the stupid movie with Kennedy and Sandy, and they barely talked to me. They shared a pop and a popcorn, and giggled together all through the previews (the best part of going to the movies!). Then they whispered really loudly in the movie, and twice I had to ask them to be quiet because it was really distracting. Sandy made some stupid remark about me being annoying to go to the movies with. Overall, it was terrible. I'm never going out with them AGAIN.

Yours truly,
Arthur Bean

▸▸ ▸▸ ▸▸

April 25th

Dear Ms Whitehead,

I hope your hip is healing and you're
able to move around now. When are you
coming back to school? We really miss
having you teach the class. I, for one,
like that you are more open to a creative
mind such as my own. Mrs. Carrell and
I have creative differences on how
English class can be interpreted, and it's
getting kind of difficult to work with her.
This whole last week we've been doing
worksheets and reading comprehension
pop quizzes. I liked that you never gave
us pop quizzes. I told Mrs. Carrell that
we didn't have to do those with you,
and she made a comment about your
teaching style being "clearly different
and maybe a little too modern." You
should make a complaint about her
criticism of you. You weren't even there
to defend yourself. I tried to defend
you, Ms Whitehead, and I got sent out
to the hall again. Anyway, I hope you
come back soon.

Yours truly,
Arthur Bean

▶▶ ▶▶ ▶▶

Assignment: Novel Response

Many works of fiction are based on the works of others. Writers will respond to another work by writing a prequel or sequel to it, or focusing on another character. For this assignment, choose a novel written by your favourite author and write a short response to it. Your response can be anything you wish: a diary entry from a secondary character, a scene starring the main character before the book starts, an epilogue about what happens afterward, etc. You will be marked on your grammar, insight and direct connection to the original novel. Ensure to clearly indicate in your title what novel you are referencing and who wrote the original piece.

Due: April 28

There will be no extensions given on this assignment.

▶▶ ▶▶ ▶▶

**Peer Tutoring Program — Progress Report
Session: April 27th
Worked On: Novel Response**

Artie helped me choose a book that I liked and we worked on an outline of a dairy response for Harris Burdick. Hes a guy whose in a book by Chris Van Allsburg but hes not really in the book he only has his name on the cover.
— Robbie

Robbie and I talked about how much better Ms Whitehead was at understanding our creative approaches to English assignments rather than being stuck with worksheets and silent reading in class. It was very collaborative.
— Arthur

Diary Entry: The Grand High Witch

By Arthur Bean

Original Novel: *The Witches* by Roald Dahl

Dear Very Evil Diary,

I, The Grand High Witch of England, am thinking of moving. I am tired of Norway and England. After this meeting of the Royal Society for the Prevention of Cruelty to Children, I will pack up all my wigs and fly across the ocean. I find the children in England have funny accents and weird words for things like candy and sweaters. Not only that, but all the children will be gone due to my Mouse-Maker potion! It's a perfect plan!

I'm thinking of moving to Canada and becoming a substitute teacher. This way I can boil children in cauldrons. Of course, I may bore them to death. That would be fun too! Anything to make their lives miserable! I will probably teach Math. Of course, I hate Math too, so that will make it even worse for the children.

My plan is to kill all the other witches who are so dumb that they can't do anything themselves, and then I can be a substitute in every school across Canada. I will use my substitute teacher powers to put my Mouse-Maker potion in the cafeteria food, and BAM! Instant Mouse School! After I torment the children with my boring Math classes, of course. It's a perfect plan!

Now I better go to sleep. I have to run a meeting in the morning.

Yours truly,
The Grand High Witch

Mr. Bean,

I am very tired of your overt displays of rebellion in your assignments. I expect that Ms Whitehead will be discussing your recent behaviour with you upon her return next week. Your lack of decorum and respect towards your superiors will not be tolerated. Principal Winter is expecting you in her office after school today.

Mrs. Carrell

▶▶ ▶▶ ▶▶

April 28th

Dear Mrs. Carrell,

I, Arthur Aaron Bean, am so very sorry for being disrespectful to you in class. I realize that even though my assignments still followed all the rules you set out, they weren't written "properly." I now understand that I should have written my assignments in the same way that everyone else wrote them and that creativity can be very subjective. I also understand that my assignments showed disrespect to you, and were also disrespectful of all my classmates. I am told that by writing differently, I somehow annoyed my classmates too, and I'm very, very sorry. I also understand that you felt that I was persecuting you

191

specifically in my last assignment. I want to assure you that I was not talking about you. I think this is clear since the high witch becomes a substitute Math teacher, and you are a substitute English teacher.

Please take this letter as my apology and that I won't do anything at all to upset you until you leave and move on to teach other students in another school far away.

Yours truly,
Arthur Bean

▶▶ ▶▶ ▶▶

April 29th

Dear RJ,

The voting is over this week for the stories. Do you think I will win? If I get published, I'll totally thank Robbie in the acknowledgements. I'll even dedicate the story to him. I've already starting dreaming about what I will do with the $200 prize money. I think I'll give some of it to my dad or buy him something nice. Easter was like this one bright spot, and now it feels like it never happened. But if I win the contest, maybe we can buy a new television or something. He's started sleeping in front of the TV all night now. He doesn't even go to bed. I've tried suggesting different activities and stuff too, but he only smiles and says things like "Another time, Champ" when I suggest that we go to a movie or something. I think I will ask Nicole if she has any suggestions about what to do. Maybe if I win the contest and the money we can go on a trip somewhere. Something fancy, with a nice hotel and a swimming pool.

Yours truly,
Arthur Bean

MAY

The "I" of the Beholder:
The Art Show Preview

By Arthur Bean

Next week the Terry Fox Jr. High cafeteria will be turned into an art gallery of the highest degree. Students from all three grades have submitted their best artwork for this public showing. The art will be up all week, with a special Art Opening for family and friends on Monday night from 6:00 to 9:00 p.m. Artists will be in attendance Monday night to answer any questions about their work and inspiration, but I had the opportunity to interview a few students about their work ahead of time.

Grade seven student Parvis Ahluwahlia has been a fan of comic books his whole life. He has drawn a series of comic strips that make humorous observations on school life. In one he has adeptly captured the horrors of eating the same food every day of the week at the cafeteria. In another, he uses humour to show the viewer the social divide between comic book nerds and jocks. His drawing style is simple and cartoonish, and his main character looks a lot like the famous Garfield the cat.

When asked about his work, Parvis said that he just draws all the time, and especially likes doodling in textbooks. He is very excited to have the chance to show off his comics in frames like real art, and is hoping that his comics will be effective in sharing their message of anti-bullying.

Parvis isn't the only comic book artist in the show. You can also see the darker worlds created by Robbie Zack, inspired by Marvel comic books.

Grade eight student Kristina Perkins prefers watercolours. Her landscapes are predominantly blue and are very peaceful.

Kristina said that she has been painting in every spare moment she has ever since she was a kid, and she likes painting pictures of her family's cottage on a lake. She says that she hopes other students find looking at her work relaxing and that her watercolours remind them of a perfect summer day. Watercolour is a popular medium this year, and you can see the whole east wall dedicated to watercolour scenes.

Finally I spoke with grade nine student Sandra Chu. Sandra says that she prefers to work with "found objects" and work them into her avant-garde sculptures. To the untrained eye, it might look like she's gluing garbage together, but she assures me that her work is very postmodern.

"I am trying to show how material goods are just being thrown away, but that we can recycle them into something meaningful for someone else," Sandra told me in her interview. "My sculptures are an attack on current government environmental policies as well as a comment on how commercialized Christmas has become."

Sandra says her main goal is to make people think differently about what is art.

These are just some of the artists who will be in attendance at what promises to be an interesting art show in the cafeteria. Come and see the rest for yourself. You won't be disappointed!

Hiya, Arthur,

Excellent work, buddy! I don't think
there's a word that needs to be
changed! You've captured the spirit
of the art show along with pertinent
facts about the show and some of the
artists. You've piqued the interest of the
reader with your insightful interviews,
and chosen three very different artists
to highlight. You've done some fantastic
work here and you should be very proud
of your article!

Cheers!
Mr. E.

▶▶ ▶▶ ▶▶

JUNIOR AUTHOR WINNER!

Terry Fox Junior High would like to congratulate
Arthur Bean on receiving the highest number
of votes for his story "Ghost Love Story"! The
results were extremely close, and we would like
to thank all the finalists for sharing their excellent
stories with us. Arthur's story will be published
in the annual junior edition of *Writers Write Now*
magazine in June, alongside the works of other
winners across the city.
Please take a minute to congratulate Arthur on
his success when you see him!

May 2nd

Dear RJ,

I won the contest. I know that I should be more
excited, but I feel so weird. It's like I ate too many
chocolates and instead of being happy, I feel
gross. I mean, I did do a lot of work on that story.
There were parts of it where it didn't make any
sense, so I changed it around, so it's practically
like I wrote it, right? It's almost like it was
Robbie's *idea*, but *I* wrote it. But then I should be
more excited. Maybe it just doesn't feel real yet. I
should probably tell my dad, but I don't even feel
like it. Do you think I will feel better when I see
my name in the magazine and get the money?

Yours truly,
Arthur Bean

From: Kennedy Laurel (imsocutekl@hotmail.com)
To: Arthur Bean (arthuraaronbean@gmail.com)
Sent: May 2, 20:03

Hi Arthur,

Congratulations on winning the competition.
   That's great for you. There's always next year for
me, I guess.

Kennedy

From: Arthur Bean (arthuraaronbean@gmail.com)
To: Kennedy Laurel (imsocutekl@hotmail.com)
Sent: May 2, 20:05

Thanks, Kennedy! It's pretty exciting! I thought your
story was really great. I wish we could have both won!

Yours truly,
Arthur ☺

Assignment: Comic Strips

First of all, I would like to thank you all for your kind words and
good wishes for my recovery. Your get-well cards kept me in
good spirits while I recuperated, and I'm very glad to be back at
school! I'm sure Mr. Fringali will be happy too, especially since
he's been walking Bruno for me while I was cooped up! All that
time watching movies and bad daytime television gave me lots of
time to think of new writing exercises for you too. I can hear you
groaning! I promise it will be fun!

I thought we would have some fun now that I'm back! Comic
books and graphic novels are often overlooked as "literature."
Write a short comic strip about a recent event in your life. It
doesn't need to be funny or long. Try to use both words and
pictures to convey the emotion of your characters. Don't
worry; I won't be marking you on the quality of your artwork,
just how you choose to blend the two together! There will be
copies of several different types of comics and graphic novels
on the Great Reads table if you are looking for examples or
inspiration.

Due: May 6

▸▸ ▸▸ ▸▸

May 3rd

Dear RJ,

Kennedy seemed so sad in school today. I
finally tried to talk to her during Gym but she
is being really weird, and it was almost like she
was avoiding even looking at me. I think she's
upset about losing the writing contest. But like
she said, there's always next year, and I told
her that her story was really good. She told me
that she just kind of wanted to forget about it.
I tried to tell her that she had other stuff going
for her too, like being Juliet in the play, but
the more I talked to her, the more upset she
seemed, and finally she told me she had to go
and ran away into the girls' change room. Her
friends told me I was being a jerk and rubbing
it in, but I told them they were wrong. I was
just trying to be nice and make her feel better
about losing. That's what I would want. It sucks
too. The first time I ever really try and talk to
her outside of rehearsals and class and stuff,
and she runs away.

Robbie's being weird too. He talks about
being in rehearsals all the time. He said that
he and Kennedy were getting together almost
every day after school to rehearse. I don't know
why Kennedy has time to run lines with him,
because she never had time to rehearse with
me. Maybe she feels sorry for him because he
needs more rehearsal time. I bet that's it. I
hope so.

With everyone being so weird I sure don't feel
any better about winning. I've been thinking of

ways to celebrate, but I can't think of anything.
I still haven't said anything to Dad or Nicole or
Luke. I don't even want to think about it, but
then I have nights like tonight when I can't sleep
and my mind won't stop thinking and I have
this knot in my stomach that won't go away.
Any ideas on how to get rid of it?

Yours truly,
Arthur Bean

▸▸ ▸▸ ▸▸

From: Arthur Bean (arthuraaronbean@gmail.com)
To: Kennedy Laurel (imsocutekl@hotmail.com
Sent: May 4, 11:16

Dear Kennedy,

I haven't talked to you much lately, and I just wanted to
say hello! I know you've been really busy with the play
and homework and stuff, but I miss hearing from you.
How are you doing? I've been pretty busy. My novel is
pretty close to being done, so that's going to be good.
It's very deep and philosophical. But I still have to write
a short story for Ms Whitehead's class. I'm glad she's
back. I hated our substitute! Anyway, I just wanted to
say hello! And May the Fourth be with you!

Yours truly,
Arthur Bean

▸▸ ▸▸ ▸▸

artie found a graphic novel version of R&J for
me to look at.

twas awesome, dost thou know it?
— Robbie

We mostly read comic books. It was a research
session.
— Arthur

▸▸ ▸▸ ▸▸

Assignment: A Day in the Life Comic Strip

By Arthur Bean

Arthur, you've done a nice job using
different sizes for emotional effect,
although this is a sadder version of your
contest win than I expected. I hope you
had some real celebrations for your
success, and perhaps learned a lesson
about the power of humility?

Ms Whitehead

From: Kennedy Laurel (imsocutekl@hotmail.com)
To: Arthur Bean (arthuraaronbean@gmail.com)
Sent: May 6, 22:43

Dear Arthur,

I know I haven't written much lately. I don't have ANYTHING good to talk about! For one thing, Sandy broke up with me. Again. He's such a jerk! I hate him sooo much! He said that I was "too busy being Kennedy that I didn't have time to be Kennedy AND Sandy."

Is that not the STUPIDEST thing you've ever heard?? It's not MY fault that he just wants to sit around the house watching TV and playing VIDEO GAMES! I actually want to DO something with my life! Can you believe him??? To think that I was in LOVE with him! GUYS SUCK! I'm done being sad about him!

Then, to top it off, my DAD spent like an HOUR telling me that I have to do better in Science! He can be such a jerk! Not EVERYONE wants to be a doctor or something! I just want to punch something!

This year sucks! I can't believe how much it sucks! I can't wait until this school year is OVER and I don't have to deal with anyone for TWO months!

K

P.S. I don't get it. What's so special about May 4th?

From: Arthur Bean (arthuraaronbean@gmail.com)
To: Kennedy Laurel (imsocutekl@hotmail.com)
Sent: May 7, 10:20

Dear Kennedy,

I'm sorry that life sucks! I hate Sandy too. I've always hated him! I'm not surprised he's being a jerk. I don't think he understands what people like you and I want in life. We are dedicated to being better people and being famous. You don't need him. Your boyfriend should be someone who understands that you like to be busy and that you are talented and fun. Your talents are wasted sitting on the couch! I mean, any guy in the school would be so lucky to have you as his girlfriend. I promise that we don't all suck — I'm a pretty good guy ☺ . . . If you want someone to talk to, I am here always for you. Maybe we can go to a movie or the mall this weekend, and we can talk about it.

Yours truly,
Arthur Bean

From: Kennedy Laurel (imsocutekl@hotmail.com)
To: Arthur Bean (arthuraaronbean@gmail.com)
Sent: May 8, 12:30

Thanks Artie. I'm totally just going to stay in my pyjamas all weekend and waste my talents on the couch LOL! I don't care! I'm taking time to be KENNEDY!
    Screw you Sandy LOL!

Kennedy ☺

From: Robbie Zack (robbiethegreat2000@hotmail.com)
To: Arthur Bean (arthuraaronbean@gmail.com)
Sent: May 8, 13:22

artie did u here that kennedy broke up with sandy?
how awesome is that??
    im totally going to make my move in rehersal
monday.
    any smooth moves u can pass on LOL?

May 8th

Dear RJ,

I need to move in on Kennedy FAST! Robbie is
going to tell her he likes her and I need to beat
him there.
    I KNEW I shouldn't have given up being
Romeo. That was so stupid, RJ! What can I do?
I tried asking her out this weekend and she said
no. So now what? I want it to be romantic and
special and show that I understand how great
she is.
    Any great ideas, RJ?

Yours truly,
Arthur Bean

▶▶ ▶▶ ▶▶

May 9th

Dear RJ,

OK, I talked to my dad and to Nicole about what
I should do. Nicole said that I should write her a
poem.

Dad said that he didn't know but he thought
the poem was a good idea. So I made a list of
words that could rhyme with Kennedy:

kennedy	*remedy*	*lemony*
heavenly	*secondly*	*tremendously*
extremity	*melody*	

As you can see, I didn't get very far.

Yours truly,
Arthur Bean

From: Kennedy Laurel (imsocutekl@hotmail.com)
To: Arthur Bean (arthuraaronbean@gmail.com)
Sent: May 9, 17:24

ARTHUR BEAN!!!!!
    How could you CHEAT like that?? Are you so low
that you STEAL from your friend?
    I can't believe I thought you were a good guy!!!
What the HELL is going on?
    YOU SUCK!!! ALL GUYS SUCK!!

From: Robbie Zack (robbiethegreat2000@hotmail.com)
To: Arthur Bean (arthuraaronbean@gmail.com)
Sent: May 9, 17:24

artie i need to talk to u cuz i might have told kennedy
today about my storey. can u call me? kennedy was
really really mad.

From: Arthur Bean (arthuraaronbean@gmail.com)
To: Robbie Zack (robbiethegreat2000@hotmail.com)
Sent: May 9, 17:26

YOU **TOLD** HER???? WHY WOULD YOU **TELL** HER???

From: Kennedy Laurel (imsocutekl@hotmail.com)
To: Arthur Bean (arthuraaronbean@gmail.com)
Sent: May 9, 18:03

AND ANOTHER THING . . .
    I'm going to tell Mr. Everett and Ms Whitehead
what you've done! I can't believe you would do this!!!
I'm just sitting here and I'm so mad I don't even know
where to start! I wish you were right HERE — I would
punch you in the face! In fact, I still might PUNCH
you! Maybe I will come to your house! Robbie
seemed SOOO upset that he told me but he should
be mad AT YOU! What were you thinking?? He said
you NEEDED it! I thought YOU wrote YOUR story!
You said that everything was perfect! You LIED to me
and you STOLE from Robbie and you CHEATED!!!
YOU ARE A TERRIBLE FRIEND!!!

From: Robbie Zack (robbiethegreat2000@hotmail.com)
To: Arthur Bean (arthuraaronbean@gmail.com)
Sent: May 9, 18:19

artie u need to answer ur phone. i need to tell u what
happenned cuz it just slipped out. r u mad at me?
u gotta call me. u gotta hear what happened. She
cornered me! I got all nervous and we were talking
and i wanted to tell her that i like her and i told her
that my storey was about her. and she was all like
"what storey" and i said "the one in the newspaper".
and she said "artie rote that storey" and i said "no
i did but i gave it to artie 4 the writing contest" and
she didnt kno that. then she got all mad and stormed
off and i still didnt tell her i like her. it was a disaster
man! call me!

From: Arthur Bean (arthuraaronbean@gmail.com)
To: Kennedy Laurel (imsocutekl@hotmail.com)
Sent: May 9, 18:22

Dear Kennedy,

I wish you would answer your phone, or text me back!
But whatever you do, please don't tell Mr. Everett and
Ms Whitehead!
    I can explain everything! I would rather explain it
in person though. It's very complicated, but there's
a good reason for it, I promise. Believe me! I never
meant to cheat! I had no other choice! I feel so
terrible! Please let me explain!

Yours truly,
Arthur Bean

May 9th

Dear RJ,

This has been the worst birthday EVER.

Yours truly,
Arthur Bean

▶▶ ▶▶ ▶▶

Assignment: What If ...
We all have a tendency to think about the "what ifs" in our lives.
I would like you to focus on one moment in your life, and think
about the "what if." Your moment can be as big as "What if my
family had moved to France?" or as small as "What if I had been
given a hamster when I was six?" Write three paragraphs as
though your "what if" had come true. How is your life different?
Has it changed for better or for worse?

Due: May 16

▶▶ ▶▶ ▶▶

From: Arthur Bean (arthuraaronbean@gmail.com)
To: Kennedy Laurel (imsocutekl@hotmail.com)
Sent: May 11, 01:24

Dear Kennedy,

I looked for you at school today but I didn't see you.
Well, that's not true. I did see you, but you seemed
really into the conversation you were having over
lunch. Then I looked for you after school, but Mr. Tan
said that you were in the theatre setting lighting

cues and couldn't be disturbed. I waited for you after rehearsal, but I didn't see you leave with everyone. I want to explain what happened with my story and the contest.

I really wanted to win. My life has sucked since Mom died and I wanted something to go right. Then the story contest came along, and I thought that I could win it and win the money and be happy! I knew your story was really great and I wanted to write a story that was as good as yours. I thought you would want to hang out with me if I was more talented.

I just couldn't write anything good. I tried. I really tried, and then one day when I was tutoring Robbie I read his story and it was everything I wanted to write! So we made a deal. I used his story in exchange for my part in *Romeo and Juliet*. You probably don't get it, but it's really important to me to win the contest and be in print. I always told my mom that I would be famous. Now that she's gone, I have to be famous so that my dad and I can live in a big house and have stuff and my dad will be happier and we won't even miss my mom at all!

I just can't write a story as good as your story right now. I loved your story. You're an amazing writer and actress and person and I can't keep up. I just want to have one thing that you have.

Anyway, I never meant for you to find out.

Yours truly,
Arthur Bean

**Peer Tutoring Program — Progress Report
Session: May 11th
Worked On: What Ifs**

What if we quit these stupid tutoring sessions?
They're a waste of time for both of us, and
Robbie doesn't need me around. He has lots
of good ideas. All he needs is spell-check on
his computer and maybe a thesaurus. I'm not
making things any better for Robbie, just more
complicated.
— Arthur

don't mind artie today. hes in a bad mood
— Robbie

May 11th

Dear RJ,

I don't understand how this could have gone so
wrong! I have no idea what Kennedy has done
or if she told anyone! I can't sleep. I should
be mad at Robbie, but he feels so bad that I
couldn't even stay mad at him. I guess one
good thing about it is that Kennedy isn't really
talking to him either. He said that in rehearsal
yesterday she just said her lines and talked
only to Mr. Tan.
    I just don't know what I should do. What
if I get suspended? Famous writers don't get
suspended from school!

Yours truly,
Arthur Bean

▶▶ ▶▶ ▶▶

From: Arthur Bean (arthuraaronbean@gmail.com)
To: Kennedy Laurel (imsocutekl@hotmail.com
Sent: May 12, 02:42

Dear Kennedy,

Did you get my email? I'm not sure if you told
anybody about my mistake with the story. No one's
said anything to me, so I hope you decided not
to tell. I would be so happy if you could just keep
it a secret. I didn't mean to make you mad at me,
and Robbie is so happy to be in the play with you.

I can't tell what you're thinking! Please just tell me what you're thinking!

Yours truly,
Arthur Bean

From: Arthur Bean (arthuraaronbean@gmail.com)
To: Kennedy Laurel (imsocutekl@hotmail.com)
Sent: May 13, 19:33

Dear Kennedy,

You must be very busy getting ready for the play since I haven't heard from you or seen very much of you at school. I will be there on opening night to see you! Maybe if you get a chance you could call to let me know that you got my last email?

Yours truly,
Arthur Bean

From: Arthur Bean (arthuraaronbean@gmail.com)
To: Kennedy Laurel (imsocutekl@hotmail.com)
Sent: May 13, 23:57

Dear Kennedy,

Please, Kennedy, please let me know what's going on. I haven't heard from you at all! I just want to talk to you!

Arthur

What If I Didn't Win the Writing Contest

By Arthur Bean

I didn't put in a story for the writing contest, because I didn't have a story to tell this year. So instead of writing a story, I tried out for the badminton team. I didn't make it onto the badminton team. I tried to start a movie club, but there weren't any teachers who wanted to give up their lunch hours to watch movies.

Luckily, I got to be in *Romeo and Juliet* anyway. I knew all my lines perfectly, and I even improvised a line that made the show better.

My performance was very moving and almost everyone in the audience was very sad when Romeo died. On stage I could hear them sniffling and blowing their noses. It was like being at a real funeral.

Then after the play, the girl playing Juliet would be so overwhelmed by my performance that she would ask me out and we would become boyfriend-girlfriend.

The saddest thing about not winning the contest is that it was my only chance to be famous really soon.

I will always wonder, *What if I won?* and I will be sad about it. I will feel like I have lost all my writing talent and I will end up working as a used car salesman or something terrible like teaching Math.

Arthur,

This is a thoughtful reflection on a recent event. You've done a nice job looking at both the positives and negatives that could happen if you did not win. However, your verb tenses are muddled. It would be best for you to choose a time frame (past, present, conditional past) and stick with it throughout.

Ms Whitehead

From: Arthur Bean (arthuraaronbean@gmail.com)
To: Kennedy Laurel (imsocutekl@hotmail.com)
Sent: May 16, 16:15

Dear Kennedy,

How are you? Robbie said that the play is almost ready and that you look hot in your costume. I can't wait to see it! He also said that you are really good at playing dead.

I would love to hear about the play from your point of view. Maybe we could do an interview for the newspaper! I could interview you! Let me know — I promise I will do a really great job!

Yours truly,
Arthur Bean

▶▶ ▶▶ ▶▶

From: Arthur Bean (arthuraaronbean@gmail.com)
To: Kennedy Laurel (imsocutekl@hotmail.com)
Sent: May 17, 20:04

Dear Kennedy,

Please talk to me! I know you're mad at me, but I really
miss you as my friend. I don't know what else to do!

Yours truly,
Arthur Bean

From: Kennedy Laurel (imsocutekl@hotmail.com)
To: Arthur Bean (arthuraaronbean@gmail.com)
Sent: May 17, 21:56

Arthur.
   STOP WRITING ME. I don't need cheaters and
losers in my life. LEAVE ME ALONE FOREVER!!!!!!

Yours ANGRILY,
Kennedy Laurel

▶▶ ▶▶ ▶▶

May 19th

Dear RJ,

Kennedy hates me. It's official. She emailed me
telling me so, and she told Catie to tell me to
leave her alone — which she did, loudly, in front
of everyone before Science today. It sucks. Now
I've lost everything, and the only person left

is Robbie Zack. He's the only person who still seems to talk to me.

I've tried everything, RJ.

I can't tell Luke what I did, because he thinks I'm pretty cool, and I don't want him to think that I'm not.

I can't tell Nicole, because she'll freak out and tell my dad.

And obviously I can't tell my dad, especially since he's actually started leaving the house again to go on walks and stuff, and I don't want to stop him from doing that.

I'm all alone in this mess. Well, all alone with you. At least you're never going to get mad at me! HAHA! You can't! You can't even talk!

But imagine how creepy it would be if you started writing back to me . . . *that* would be an awesome horror story!

Yours truly,
Arthur Bean

▶▶ ▶▶ ▶▶

Assignment: Spring Has Sprung!

With spring come all kinds of changes in the world. I love planting my garden and seeing the lilacs come into bloom!

Write a descriptive paragraph about spring. Look around you on your walk home after school or around your house or the school. What are some of the things that you observe with the coming of spring?

Due: May 24

▶▶ ▶▶ ▶▶

May 21

Arthur Bean
Apt. 16, 155 Tormy Street
Calgary, AB

Writers Write Now Magazine
PO Box 134 Stn M
Calgary, AB

To whom it may concern,

There has been a mistake in the authorship of the
winning entry for Terry Fox Junior High for the
Junior Authors contest.

My name, Arthur Aaron Bean, has been attached
to the story "Ghost Love Story."

The real author is actually Robert Zack, although
I helped him a lot with it, so my name should
probably be mentioned too.

The author should probably read: *written by Robert
Zack with help from Arthur Bean.*

Yours truly,
Arthur Bean

Spring

By Arthur Bean

When spring comes, the windows get opened at home. The air is crisp and seeps into the couch and chair, and even though it's still too cold to open the windows, we do it anyway. My dad and I have to have blankets up to our chins to watch television, but neither of us will be the one to suggest closing the window. The living room feels brighter somehow. Maybe it's because the laundry gets put out on the balcony rather than blocking the fireplace and the dining room.

Spring smells.

It's like the whole city has turned into a farm. My dad says it's the wind coming off the farms outside the city, but I'm pretty sure it's just all the dog turds that people didn't pick up over the winter thawing out and getting stepped in.

This spring there is a change happening. Nicole convinced my dad to sign up for some kind of yoga class, even though he's never done yoga before. Nicole got a boyfriend and she says she's in love. Pickles has disappeared again, but you can still see some of her paw prints in the leftover snow outside the apartment building, so I know she's close by. She's so annoying, but I still like having her around.

I only have one sleeve left to finish on the sweater I'm knitting. I wish my mom were here to see me wear it.

Dear Arthur,

I enjoyed how you focused on the changes that happen in your apartment and not just on the natural changes happening outside.
    I appreciated your honest and straightforward description. I hope you finish your sweater soon; I would love to see it!

Ms Whitehead

REMINDER:

Your short stories (that we began back in February) are due on June 6; that's just two weeks away. I'm certain you have all been working hard on your stories, and I'm sure none of you will be writing frantically this weekend (hint hint). Feel free to speak to me if you have any questions, and please make sure to spell-check and proofread your story before handing it in!
Ms Whitehead

May 24th

Dear RJ,

All I do these days is write about things that I don't want to write about. I wonder if famous authors ever hate writing too. Although, at least they get millions of dollars to do it.

Yours truly,
Arthur Bean

▶▶ ▶▶ ▶▶

May 25

Writers Write Now Magazine
PO Box 134 Stn M
Calgary, AB

Arthur Bean
Apt. 16, 155 Tormy Street
Calgary, AB

Dear Mr. Bean,

We have received your letter regarding the authorial change on the Terry Fox Junior High submission for the "Junior Authors" edition of *WWN* magazine. In order to make such a change, we need a letter from the school, as well as a letter of affirmation from Robert Zack that he co-wrote "Ghost Love Story." These letters may be emailed as attachments, and must be received before June 10 for the change to be made before the magazine goes to print.

Should you have any questions, please don't hesitate to contact me during business hours. My contact information is below.

Sincerely,

Erin Kennedy

Erin Kennedy
Editor, *WWN* Magazine
Ph: (222) 539-8909
Email: (erin.w.kennedy@gmail.com)

▸▸ ▸▸ ▸▸

May 27th

Dear RJ,

Why is nothing easy? I try and do the right
thing, and now it's even harder. I just want
to disappear. It wouldn't be hard. I don't have
anything left. I gave Robbie credit for his story
AND my role as Romeo. Kennedy won't talk to
me. Ms Whitehead expects a story for class.

I did notice that a girl who has Kennedy's
name manages the magazine. That's a sign that
I'm doing the right thing, isn't it? I stole a piece
of letter paper from the office today so that I can
send in a letter. I bet a lot of that paper goes
missing. I'm surprised they just leave it beside
the printer. Kids could totally make new report
cards if they wanted to.

Yours truly,
Arthur Bean

▶▶ ▶▶ ▶▶

Peer Tutoring Program — Progress Report
Session: May 30th
Worked On: Story Ideas

first we worked on my graphic story, and artie
helped me come up with a title. Im going to
call it "Mosquito Plague" because its all about
bugs invading peoples beds while they sleep and
getting into their brains through their eyes and
makeing them act like mosquitoes.

Then i helped artie try and come up with some ideas for his storey for class because he needed help not me. tables have turned haha
— Robbie

I concur.
— Arthur Bean

JUNE

June 3rd

Dear Ms Whitehead,

I don't have a story for our short story
assignment. I have the ideas for a lot
of stories, but I can't make them work
when I try to write them. I think they
all suck. I tried to write something, but
I don't have any stories left in me. I'm
sorry to let you down.

Yours truly,
Arthur Bean

Dear Arthur,

I wish you had spoken to me sooner
about your short story assignment
rather than waiting until the Friday
before the due date.

In the future, please come see me
sooner when you have difficulties with
the assignment.

That being said, I'm sorry to hear
that you feel that way about your

stories. I think you show real promise in being a writer, and it can be very difficult to get started (or get finished). Even famous writers often get bogged down in their own ideas, or question their work. Arthur, you are an excellent writer. Your poems are well crafted, you think creatively and you have a razor-sharp wit. Your story for the writing contest was one of the few that I read, but it was very well written. I can accept that story for your assignment.

Keep your chin up, Arthur! You still have the weekend to work on something. I know that writing can be very daunting, but keep moving forward!

Ms Whitehead

Dear Ms Whitehead,

I don't want to use that story for my assignment. I don't think it shows off my best qualities. I would rather take a zero.

Yours truly,
Arthur Bean

Arthur, your story does not have to be long; a few pages will be plenty! Why don't you make a list of your story ideas, and we can discuss fleshing one of your ideas out into something more. Sometimes it helps to talk something through with another person to know what you want to say or where you want your story to go. Come see me after class and we can discuss this. I don't believe that you don't have a story in you!

Ms Whitehead

Story Ideas

By Arthur Bean

See, Ms Whitehead? I've got nothing.

▶▶ ▶▶ ▶▶

June 6th

To Whom It May Concern,

Please excuse Arthur Bean from school tomorrow.

Thank you,
Ernie Bean

▸▸ ▸▸ ▸▸

June 7th

Dear RJ,

Today is the anniversary of the day that Mom died. I didn't go to school today. I thought Dad would want to go to the cemetery again, but he didn't. He just went to some meditation class. He just left me here in the apartment alone. I thought dads were supposed to pay attention to their kids, not just do whatever they wanted. Why should I have to stay here by myself, totally alone?? What am I supposed to do today?? Why should I have to be by myself on the worst day of the year??? I hate him!!! I don't even want to be a person today. I would rather be a bug or something with no memory or even consciousness. Is it tomorrow yet?

Yours truly,
Arthur Bean

From: Robbie Zack (robbiethegreat2000@hotmail.com)
To: Arthur Bean (arthuraaronbean@gmail.com)
Sent: June 7, 19:52

artie u didnt sho for tutoring and i think i kno why.
dude, i kno its not ok that ur mom is gone cuz it cant
ever be ok. But if u want to play minecraft this week u
can come hear if u want.

▶▶ ▶▶ ▶▶

June 8th

Dear RJ,

I thought today would be a little better, but
it's not. And now my dad is creeping around
the house really quietly because I yelled at
him yesterday and he doesn't know what to
do either. So even though I didn't think it was
possible, I feel even worse for making him feel
bad. I know he is sad too. I think our sadnesses
are too different from each other to really be sad
together. Is that possible? Can two people miss
the same person in different ways?
    RJ, I don't know what I want to do. I thought
it would be OK by now. It's been a whole year.
But you know what, RJ? Robbie is right. It's
never going to be OK. I just hope it can be
easier. I can't be sad my whole life, can I? Maybe
this year was just meant to suck. I don't even
believe in fate, but I've got to put it down to
something. So today, I'm going to believe in fate.

Yours truly,
Arthur Bean

From: Arthur Bean (arthuraaronbean@gmail.com)
To: Erin Kennedy (erin.w.kennedy@gmail.com)
Sent: June 8, 20:26

Dear Mrs. Erin Kennedy,
    Here are the two letters that you need to change my name on "Ghost Love Story" to Robbie's name. One is an email, and the other is a real letter on real school letterhead.

Yours truly,
Arthur Bean

Attachments included: **email**; **letter**

From: Robbie Zack (robbiethegreat2000@hotmail.com)
To: Arthur Bean (arthuraaronbean@gmail.com)
Sent: June 8, 19:11

artie — Here is ur email saying that I wrote Ghost Love Storey. I wrote it and u edited it and stuff. Is that what u need? i didnt really know what u need it 4. Do u want a seequel LOL?
    Also, r u going to the dance next friday? can ur dad give me a ride home? my dad said that he has a date that nite. can you believe that guy, having a girl friend after my mom left already??? he must be really good-looking. i must get my charm from him!

robbie

Terry Fox Junior High

103 Camirand Drive, Calgary AB
Ph: (222) 274-7547
"Where perseverance meets excellence"

June 8

Writers Write Now Magazine
PO Box 134 Stn M
Calgary, AB

Dear Erin Kennedy,

Please accept this letter as evidence that Terry Fox
Junior High, "where perseverance meets excellence,"
is aware of the author change on our submission
for the Junior Authors edition of *Writers Write Now*
magazine. The author of "Ghost Love Story" is
Robert Zack, with help from Arthur Bean. Thank
you for making this change last minute. Remember
that both names could still be published on the story
if you want.

Yours truly,
Ms A. Whitehead
An English Teacher

▸▸ ▸▸ ▸▸

June 13th

Dear RJ,

I asked Mr. Everett if I could review *Romeo and Juliet* this week. This is my chance to apologize and show Kennedy how much she means to me. I hope she's good, because I'm really tired of lying. I also sent stuff to the magazine. I guess it's OK. I'm kind of glad that my first story with only my name on it will be my real story, not someone else's. I actually feel a little better, even better than when I won.

I wonder if Kennedy will like me again when she sees that I fixed it. I hope so. I mean, I didn't really have to fix it. Robbie said that I should send her a bouquet too, but I looked when we were at the store and flowers are so expensive! I guess I'd better do that though. I have to do something nice!

Also, I came home today, and there were a couple of new books on my bed. One was about writing novels, and one was a knitting for guys book. My dad didn't say anything, but I thanked him anyway. They both look pretty cool, and he said that he bookmarked the tuque he wants me to make for him.

Yours truly,
Arthur Bean

▸▸ ▸▸ ▸▸

June 14th

Dear Ms Whitehead,

I never handed in a story, but I think
I have something that I can do. Is it
OK if I hand in something this week? I
know I said I would take a zero, but I'm
pretty sure that real writers wouldn't
do that. Maybe you won't even take any
marks off because it will be so good!

Yours truly,
Arthur Bean

Arthur,

Of course, I will accept your late
submission. I'm glad that you were
able to find some inspiration this week.
Please note, though, that I will have to
deduct some marks for tardiness. It's
only fair to the rest of the class. I look
forward to reading your story.

Ms Whitehead

▸▸ ▸▸ ▸▸

A Standing Ovation for *Romeo and Juliet*

By Arthur Bean

Terry Fox Jr. High was treated to the saddest version of *Romeo and Juliet* ever performed this past weekend. The Drama Club has been working on the production for most of the winter, and their hard work has definitely paid off.

First off, the set was cool. Mr. Tan decided to set the play like it was today, and so the set looked like two colourful apartment buildings, complete with the balconies needed for a proper version of *Romeo and Juliet*. The chorus changed the scenes efficiently, using black cloth to create the tomb and the scenes with the friars. The contrast of colours to black also set the mood of the scenes very well.

Also, the acting was very realistic. Mr. Tan had a small cast who split many of the smaller roles. Through costume changes and a change in the way they walked, each character was very recognizable, even for audience members who have never read the play, like my dad. Benjamin Crisp was hilarious as the nurse, especially when there was a costume problem and his skirt fell off. His quick wit and improv skills really came in handy.

But no one could steal the show from the very talented Kennedy Laurel, who played Juliet. She spoke her lines as though they were written today, and made the audience truly believe that she loved Romeo. It was hard to believe that the girl in the ball gown is the same athlete who is so competitive on the volleyball court. Robbie Zack (Romeo) was easy to understand, and he was really good in his role, especially since he didn't start rehearsals until April. Their scenes together were strong and believable, and the audience was very sad when they both died at the end. Even my dad cried a little bit, although he said it was just hay fever. It was a five-star performance from the Drama Club, and for those of us lucky enough to have seen one (or all) of the three sold-out performances, it was a play to be remembered.

*Excellent review, Arthur! I'm glad to
see that you were able to be so objective
about the play. With one issue of the
Marathon left, would you like to write
an article on your experiences this year?
I was thinking a kind of quirky "year in
review" opinion piece. Why don't we call
it "Arthur Unknown"? Cheers!*

Mr. Everett

▶▶ ▶▶ ▶▶

From: Kennedy Laurel (imsocutekl@hotmail.com)
To: Arthur Bean (arthuraaronbean@gmail.com)
Sent: June 16, 18:05

Dear Arthur,

Thanks for your glowing review of *Romeo and Juliet*.
You wrote really kind things and it was nice to read
it. Also thank you for the bouquet. The roses were a
surprise on my dressing-room table, and your card was
sweet. At first I thought they were from Sandy LOL!
  I still think what you did was really wrong. Robbie
told me that you fixed it in the magazine, which was
the only right thing to do. Still, I can't believe you
would do that in the first place! Next year you HAVE
to be my partner in the competition so that I KNOW
that you aren't cheating!
  Anyway, thanks for the review and the flowers. I
really liked both of them, and I accept your apology
on the card.

Kennedy ☺

From: Arthur Bean (arthuraaronbean@gmail.com)
To: Kennedy Laurel (imsocutekl@hotmail.com)
Sent: June 16, 18:26

Dear Kennedy,

I'm so glad you liked the flowers! They were really expensive too! My dad said that roses were my mom's favourite flower and he helped me find the perfect ones! I really meant everything on the card. I think you did amazing and I'm sorry to have let you down. You were great as Juliet, and I really believed that you and Robbie were in love. So you must be a great actress, right? Hahaha. You aren't dating Robbie though, are you? I mean, you guys are still just friends, right?

Maybe you and me and Robbie can go to a movie or something together as friends? I think that could be really fun. My dad can probably drive us there. He's been going to yoga almost every night and his studio is right by the movie theatre.

Yours truly,
Arthur Bean

▶▶ ▶▶ ▶▶

June 17th

Dear Ms Whitehead,

Here is my short story. Thank you for the extension and for helping me find a story. It was nice of you to do that.

Yours truly,
Arthur Bean

The Ballad of the Cat Thief

By Arthur Bean

This is the ballad of Artie the Witty,
The evil Frank Dack and Pickles the kitty
And a rescue so daring it made it to lore
(But don't worry, ladies, there will be no gore).

Frank wants Artie's cat and he wants her so badly
She reminds him too much of his now dead cat
Bradley.
Listen up now to our kitty tale's genesis.
(You must understand
that this guy's Artie's nemesis.)

Because Frank is evil, he does some quick plotting
And steals away Pickles without anyone spotting!
He shows Pickles to Sophie, the girl of his dreams
Whose love of cute kittens makes her coo,
squeal and scream!

But Artie is ruined! He can't get more sad.
(It's not looking good for this good-looking lad.)
The weekend goes by; Artie sinks in despair.
His cat has gone missing. The world is not fair!

But come Monday morning while walking to school
Artie hears a faint noise from the house by the pool.
He stops for a minute — by golly, it's true!
That sound is from Pickles! He can tell by her "mew"!

He checks out the mailbox . . . Frank Dack lives inside!
Artie's got so fired up that his insides feel fried!
He must find a way to get his kitty cat back!
He stops and he thinks and he plans his attack!

Artie waits until night and sneaks into Frank's house.
He's dressed as a ghost and as quiet as a mouse.
He stands in the hall while he wails and he moans.
He jiggles door handles and wavers his tones.

He plays with the curtains and throws stuff around,
But Frank is unswayed by the spookiest sounds.
"You're not really a ghost!" he calls out to the hall.
"I know you're a person who's stupid and small.

"To whoever it is who is under that sheet,
It's time for your break-in to turn and retreat.
I'll call the police if you don't leave right now . . . "
Arties runs from the house, a sad hand to his brow.

He stays up all night, worried, fretting and thinking.
It seems as though all of his options are shrinking.
He slips into a dream as the sun starts its rising
And then WHAMMO! It hits him so hard
                    it's surprising.

His new plan is brilliant! His success is assured.
His methods are shady but his motives are pure!
He's armed with some cat food
            — Pickles' favourite brand
And a net that he knit for the rescue at hand . . .

Artie whistles for Pickles, and Pickles looks down
Where she sees her old owner and responds with
                    a "Meown."
Artie opens the cat food so the scent can waft up
And Pickles smells scents of her old favourite sup.

Artie opens his knitting to create a safe drop
(Even with her nine cat lives, the ground's
                    a hard stop).
He motions to Pickles to trust him and jump
And then the cat's flying! She lands with a "Whump!"

It's Pickles and Artie! They've been reunited!
And Frank's kitty-napping has been rightly smited!
And not only that, but the rescue is seen
By Sophie, the lover and beauty teen queen.

She watches as Pickles flies high like a dove
And then she sees Artie and falls madly in love,
For all ladies love a grand lad who can knit,
A lad who's well-rounded, with resource and wit.

They patent his net, Artie's cat-saving sweater
And then after that, life just couldn't get better!
(And as for that Frank guy, he's now learned
his lesson
And works frenching fries at a delicatessen.)

The End

Dear Arthur,

You've written a charming story poem!
Your sense of humour shines through
and your rhymes are nicely varied. I'm
glad you found a way to "knit" together
some elements of your own life into your
plot line. Well done!

Ms Whitehead

▶▶ ▶▶ ▶▶

June 20th

Dear RJ,

I have come to a very important conclusion. I, Arthur Aaron Bean, am a man of few words. I don't need long, drawn-out sentences to adequately describe a scene or a character or a plot. I don't need paragraphs to pull my readers in.

I am a poet. My stories can be told in short bursts. In fact, my stories are stronger that way. I might be the next great American poet, like Alfred Tennyson and William Blake. My work will be read in classrooms for years to come, I bet. They'll say things about how my work centres on real-world problems and how I came from a difficult background but overcame everything for my art, I bet.

Do you think poets make a lot of money?

Yours truly,
Arthur Bean

From: Arthur Bean (arthuraaronbean@gmail.com)
To: Kennedy Laurel (imsocutekl@hotmail.com)
cc: Robbie Zack (robbiethegreat2000@hotmail.com)
Sent: June 20, 15:50

Dear Kennedy,

I never heard back from you about maybe going to the movies with Robbie and me.

I asked Robbie about it and he's really excited about going — you know, as friends.

Anyway, let us know! We'll even treat you!

Yours truly,
Arthur Bean

▶▶ ▶▶ ▶▶

Ongoing Reading Journals

Remember the reading journals you began in September? Although these are for personal responses to your reading, I would like to see that you've done some reflections. Please bring your journals in to show your work. You have a bit of time to polish up your journal if you wish, or to redact specific pages (which is hiding pages you may not be comfortable sharing with me if they have some personal thoughts — you can tape them shut, or staple them together). I look forward to reading about your reading!

Due: June 23

June 21st

Dear RJ,

Ms Whitehead wants us to *hand in* our reading journals? I can't hand you in! What would you do without me? I don't think I should hand you in. You and I, we've been through a lot together this year. Plus, even though Ms Whitehead says she won't read the private stuff, I think she will. She's nosy like that. As if she wouldn't want to know the private thoughts of her students. If I were a teacher, I would totally read the whole thing! I'm going to have to tape almost every page shut. I hope she just thinks I read a bunch of books. I'll write some fake entries to add to you, starting . . . NOW!

Yours truly,
Arthur Bean

November 30th

Dearest Reading Journal,

I read a few novels this month that Luke sent me. Luke is my cousin who reads a lot. They were all science fiction novels. I thought most of them were OK, but I don't really like books that take place in outer space. I know that must be weird, since all nerds like *Star Trek*. It must prove my utter coolness . . . HA!

Anyway, once I got over the space parts, the stories were pretty good. There was a lot of fighting, and then there were a bunch of weird alien sex scenes. I mostly skipped those parts. In the end Captain Mark Freeloader won the freedom of the universe. What kind of last name is Freeloader? I get that the guy is always borrowing stuff from other species and not giving it back, but it's still a bit obvious, don't you think? The girl in the book was named Guidonna. I guess it's like a female version of Guido. You can make a female version of anything! When I read that, I decided that I'm going to call my next character Franklina. Or maybe I'll call her Arthura, although that sounds like a body part, or maybe an exotic disease. I bet that Guidonna contracts Arthura in the next Mark Freeloader book, and he has to visit a hostile planet to get the antidote. I bet they make movies out of the books. I would watch the movies probably. As long as they don't have Richard Gere in them. My mom loved his movies, but I think he's boring.

One book that I can tell you I won't be reading is the book that Auntie Deborah gave me. *You Need Rain to Make Flowers — a Manual for Grief.* I'm going to leave it in the rain and see if I get roses from it. Ha! It looks so boring that sometimes when I can't sleep, I just look at it and bam! Snoozeland! It works better than my Math textbook.

I read so much that I don't even think this reading journal will be able to keep up. In fact, just this week I read three books. I'm a very fast reader. My mom said that I was basically a speed reader, but she didn't believe that I was actually reading all the words or even cared about the plot. But I'm just fast!

I think that next month I'm going to read only important books. There are so many novels where the back cover or one of the blurbs about the book says "This is an important book." Since my own books will be important books, I should probably read a few and see what I need to do. Who decides they are important, I wonder? Do important books mean that lives have changed by reading those novels? That's what I want to happen to my readers. I'll probably write in this reading journal all about how my life has

changed by the books I've read. This reading
journal will likely be deeply personal (another
of my favourite sayings that are written on book
jackets!) and my responses will evoke so much
emotion! It will be like the time that my mom
read this book about a kid whose dad died in
the Twin Towers and she cried for hours, even
though she had finished the book already! But
I don't cry at books. Maybe that's another sign
that I haven't been reading deeply personal,
important books. Ha!

Yours truly,
Arthur Bean

▶▶ ▶▶ ▶▶

Assignment: Conclusions/Alternate Endings

As we reach the conclusion of our year together, it's time to learn
how to wrap up a good story. The conclusion of any great story
doesn't need to say it all, but it does need to tie up most of your
loose ends, and perhaps leave your reader wanting more, or
feeling happy with where you have left your characters (the best
writers are able to do both at the same time!).

In this assignment I would like you to take a well-known fairy
tale and rewrite the ending. As you know, all fairy tales end with
a "happily ever after." Maybe Cinderella doesn't get to try on the
shoe; then what would happen? Maybe the woodsman doesn't
save Red Riding Hood, or perhaps the Gingerbread Man breaks
a leg. Can you find a new and creative ending to a well-known
story?

Due: June 27

▶▶ ▶▶ ▶▶

artie and i killed off every prince charming ever created today. it was awsome!
— Robbie

Robbie and I both felt that the most effective endings are when the bad guys die. In the end, we felt that us killing off all the Prince Charmings would be better for all girls out there waiting for their prince. Robbie and I are both happy to jump into that role for any young, beautiful princesses who are rich and have their own cars.
— Arthur Bean

▶▶ ▶▶ ▶▶

It's Arthur Unknown!

By Arthur Bean

Hello, Fans and Readers!

Welcome to my new column, an extremely entertaining observation of the world at Terry Fox Junior High!

I've been asked to write a reflective "year in review" article of my opinion of starting in junior high.

I'd like to start with the grade nines. Why do they not know who any of the grade sevens are? I'm certain that I recognize the whole graduating class, but when I say hi to them in the grocery store or wherever I might be, they look at me like I'm a total stranger. That's weird. Maybe I should follow them around and find out what they are buying. Next time I can tell you who buys laxatives or zit cream! Watch out, grade nines!

I also think that our uniforms are really ugly. Blue and gold? Did they buy them at Ikea? At least our track and field team placed last in our division this year. If they had been actually fast, they would look like someone was sick after drinking Kool-Aid and eating lemon birthday cake! Maybe next year there will be real runners on the team!

There are a few things lacking as well from our school. I didn't expect to have to put up with the horrible smells coming from the grade eight Home Ec unit on homestyle cooking! Hamburger soup? More like Hamburger Poop, I say!

I have so many more observations, but I'd rather save some of them for next school year. Keep your eyes on this space for the next *Arthur Unknown*!

Hiya, Arthur,

Yowza! I'm going to hold this article back from printing; it's not exactly what I had in mind. I'm a bit worried that you could get beat up if we publish these observations! The biggest thing to remember: you don't need to try to be funny! Your wit comes across in your regular articles, and I know what you were trying to do here, but it doesn't really work. What I think you meant to be witticisms read more to an outsider as insults. It's just kind of mean instead of funny.

I was hoping you would share your
fears and worries with your readers;
you're a good guy, so I'm sure they
would delight in your triumphs and feel
bad for your failures. We can talk more
about this in the new school year (I hope
you stay part of the Newspaper Club in
September!)
Have a great summer, Arthur!

Cheers!
Mr. E.

▶▶ ▶▶ ▶▶

From: Kennedy Laurel (imsocutekl@hotmail.com)
To: Arthur Bean (arthuraaronbean@gmail.com)
cc: Robbie Zack (robbiethegreat2000@hotmail.com)
Sent: June 26, 21:12

Dear Arthur AND Robbie!

Sorry I didn't get back to you about the movie! I've
been CRAZY busy! AND my family is going away for
the summer. We're going to Malaysia for my dad's
work. DON'T ASK WHY! (We go every year! We
even have a house that we rent! It's SO HOT LOL!)
Normally we have a pretty good time when we go
away, but this year it seems to be TERRIBLE! My
brother doesn't want to come at all, and my dad is
forcing him to come on a family vacation! I think it
might be the WORST idea ever!

Also, did I tell you that I have a new boyfriend!
He's my next door neighbour's babysitter's brother
— so complicated, I know LOL! ANYWAY, I've been

seeing him lots! I asked him if he wanted to go to the movies with us and he thought that sounded fun! Plus he wants to meet Robbie . . . the boy who kissed me in front of the WHOLE school LOL! He says that he's jealous of him! Watch out Robbie . . . he plays football LOL!!!

Maybe we can go on the last day of school, like an end of the year celebration!

Let me know!

Kennedy ☺

From: Robbie Zack (robbiethegreat2000@hotmail.com)
To: Arthur Bean (arthuraaronbean@gmail.com)
Sent: June 26, 22:35

did u get k's response? i hate that guy all ready. i worked all year 4 her to like me.

From: Arthur Bean (arthuraaronbean@gmail.com)
To: Robbie Zack (robbiethegreat2000@hotmail.com)
Sent: June 26, 22:37

Totally. I concur.

Arthur

▶▶ ▶▶ ▶▶

From: Arthur Bean (arthuraaronbean@gmail.com)
To: Kennedy Laurel (imsocutekl@hotmail.com)
cc: Robbie Zack (robbiethegreat2000@hotmail.com)
Sent: June 27, 22:42

Dear Kennedy,

I'm glad that you are able to celebrate the end of
school with us. I guess since your boyfriend is coming
he can pay for you! That means Robbie and I can get
popcorn!

Let's talk at school about what movie to see
tomorrow. See you in Gym.

Yours truly,
Arthur Bean

▸▸ ▸▸ ▸▸

The Princess and the Frog
— Alternate Ending

By Arthur Bean

"No, you must kiss me!" pleaded the frog with
the frightened princess.

"Ew! No!" she squealed and threw the frog
against the wall of her bedroom. He hit the pink
painted wall with a loud *thud*, and slid to the
ground. Then the most magical thing happened.
The frog began to grow and transform, until he
was the size of a real human man. The princess
was shocked.

The prince, though, looked a bit . . . funny. His
cape was not in the princely colour of purple,
but was solid black with red underneath. His

hair was not tousled and curly, but slicked
back against his head and very oily. He was
unnaturally pale too, and his teeth were sharp
and coming out of his mouth.

"You're . . . you're . . . a . . . " the princess
whispered.

"A vampire," the prince finished grandly. "The
Prince of Darkness, at your service."

"But you said that you were a prince under an
evil spell!"

"Did I? I'm a little dyslexic. I meant that I'm
evil, under a prince's spell." The prince smiled.

The princess thought back to the pond where
they had met. She gasped. "All those dead frogs
and fish . . . that was *you*??"

The prince nodded. "And you thought they
were an environmental thing like acid rain or
whatever," he chuckled. "Oh, girls. You can be so
stupid!" Then in a flash he had her by the throat.
"But you know, darling . . . princesses taste the
sweetest . . . " and he bit into her neck with a
hungry sigh.

The End

Arthur,

I was definitely surprised by your ending
choice for this classic tale. Do you think
that it matches with the style of the
rest of the tale?

Ms Whitehead

▶▶ ▶▶ ▶▶

December 1st

Dear Reading Journal,

I read 17 books in the Mark Freeloader series
this month. Like I said, I'm a really fast reader.
Luke said that I should read the "Hitchhiker"
series next. I don't know what this is, but I'm
hoping that it's a true story about a couple who
is travelling alone at night, and they pick up a
hitchhiker, but then the hitchhiker vanishes
before they get to the next town. One of Luke's
friends' dads had that happen to him once. So
creepy . . . Not that I believe in ghosts. It was
probably Captain Mark Freeloader saving the
world in book 18! Ha!

Yours truly,
Arthur Bean

January 2nd

Dear Reading Journal,

I read a lot of books over the holidays. The worst
book was *Chicken Soup for the Teenage Soul.* My
aunt gave it to me because she thought it would
be soothing or something. I think it should be
called *Puke for the Teenage Soul*, because that's
what it made me want to do.

Yours truly,
Arthur Bean

March 1st

Dear Reading Journal,

I've been reading a lot of books on acting since I'll be starring in the play. *Pretending to Be Someone Else* was the best. I don't normally like non-fiction books, but sometimes you have to read them to learn stuff. A couple have really good tips on acting. For one thing, I learned a tip on seeming really drunk. To act drunk you just pretend that you have a ball on the top of your head and that you have to keep it there no matter where you walk. This makes you move your head more and take funny steps. I am going to try acting drunk today in rehearsal, which will work for the scene since I will have been at a ball so I probably had a beer.

Yours truly,
Arthur Bean

June 1st

Dear Reading Journal,

I've been reading graphic novels because Robbie likes them. I used to think they were for kids, but they're really cool. Robbie even thought maybe we would write one together, but I can't draw. I guess Robbie could draw and I could write. Or at least I could check his grammar . . . HA!

Yours truly,
Arthur Bean

Dear Arthur,

Wow! The sheer number of pages you've filled in your journal is impressive. Is this perhaps why you handed it in late?

I think it's wonderful that you were able to connect so deeply with what you were reading. So deeply that you've taped practically the whole journal together. It's strange that many of the only entries left for me to read are the ones you've written on the first of the month, and also seem to be taped in over other work . . .

I'm also confused; you may not know this, but I'm an avid science fiction reader (something we have in common!). I went looking for this mysterious "Captain Mark Freeloader" series you speak so highly of, but strangely, I can't find it online or at the library. It's very odd that such a prolific series (18 books!) is so underground, don't you think? Any thoughts on these anomalies in your reading journal?

Ms Whitehead

Dear Ms Whitehead,

I don't think it's that strange. To be honest, I accidentally left my journal at Nicole's, and I couldn't find it anywhere. But I knew how important it was to keep writing, so I kept it separately. I strive to be the best student, and all the other stuff I taped over is just Nicole's scribbles and recipes and stuff. She had no idea it was a class assignment.

And Captain Mark Freeloader is very underground. Actually, you have to subscribe to a mailing list to get the books, and then you have to send them back again as soon as you're done. I would give you the address, but I had to promise Luke that I would never give it out, since he was never supposed to give it to me. So now you know my secret. Don't tell anyone you know about The Captain!

Yours truly,
Arthur Bean

Well, Arthur, I hope you got <u>something</u> out of the reading journal assignment. We'll both have to make sure that such a thing doesn't happen again next year. Maybe the lesson for you this year is to keep better track of your belongings. Next year, I expect to see more in-depth entries

I appreciate your "honesty" — and I'll make sure that nothing about Captain Mark Freeloader ever gets out. If it becomes a hit, it won't be because of you or me spilling the beans!

Ms Whitehead

June 29th

Dear RJ,

Last day of school tomorrow!

Dad asked me if he should sign me up for arts camp this summer. He said that a woman at his work suggested it, since her daughter used to go and really liked it. There goes my dream trip to Australia. Maybe it's for the best. I'd hate to be eaten by a shark, so far away from home. Arts camp could be cool, but I don't know. I've never been to camp before. This one has writing and painting and Dad said that they even have video cameras for us to use. I actually think I would make a really great film director. I could be the next Steven Spielberg or Ed Wood! Plus, it turns out that Robbie is going to the same camp, so that might be OK. Wait! Unless he's planning to kill me, like the guy in our story . . . Great. Now I'm going to have to stay away from the lake.

I wish Kennedy was going to be there, but she is leaving this weekend for Malaysia. At least, I think that's what she said. She was crying a lot. I think she also mentioned that she was going to miss her boyfriend. It was kind of a lame goodbye. Girls are so weird sometimes. I think she said she would write to me. Or at least, she said she would write *back* to me. Does that mean she'll be thinking of me from across the world? I hope arts camp has a good rhyming dictionary for my poetry.

My dad is going to camp too. He signed up for this wilderness yoga retreat. It sounded terrible to me. He has to do yoga three or four times a day and all this meditation in between. Not only

254

that, but all the food is vegetarian. I hope arts
camp has hamburgers. Artists eat burgers, right?

I want to take you with me, RJ, but I don't
know if I'll have room in my backpack. Plus,
I don't want Robbie getting his hands on you.
So I might start a new RJ. I won't call him
RJ though, I promise. Maybe AJ, for Arthur's
Journal. I think you guys will get along, as
much as journals can talk HA!

Yours truly,
Arthur Bean

▶▶ ▶▶ ▶▶

Dear Arthur,

We've come to the end of our year
together and I must say, it's been a
learning experience for me too, teaching
you and watching you grow! You are
certainly creative in all your work. I
hear that I will have you in my class
next year. Since you already have a
distinct writing voice, we'll focus on
directing your writing properly, and
strengthening your organizational skills
too. I expect that grade eight will hold
more creative challenges for both of
us! Have a great summer; read lots of
books, and write your heart out!

Sincerely,
Ms Whitehead

Dear Ms Whitehead,

I get it, and I don't blame you. It can be hard to work with kids as gifted as I am. It's a blessing and a curse really.

Yours truly,
Arthur Bean

YEAR-END REPORT CARD

Arthur was a pleasure to have in class. He participated actively in discussions and showed a keen interest in the materials studied. Arthur needs to work on meeting deadlines, respecting teacher authority and allowing others the opportunity to share their opinions in class. I look forward to teaching him next year. Have a great summer!

Year-End Summary attached.

Arthur Bean
English 7A — Ms Whitehead
Year-End Summary

My Introduction	*82%*
Letter to My Future Self	*80%*
Elegies and Odes	*64%*
Acrostic Poem	*79%*
Call and Response Poem	*73%*
Remembrance Day Poem	*63%*
Shakespearean Reflection	*75%*
A Midsummer Night's Dream Diary	*61%*
Holiday Free-Form Writing Exercise	*89%*
Character Sketch	*89%*
Interview a Friend	*60%*
Interview About Me	*78%*
Dramatic Scene	*77%*
Conflict	*65%*
Reading Comprehension Worksheet	*42%*
Limerick	*49%*
Famous Author Biography	*51%*
Novel Response	*53%*
Comic Strip	*83%*
What If . . .	*80%*
Spring Free-Writing Exercise	*87%*
Final Short Story Assignment	*75%*
Conclusions/Alternate Endings	*82%*
Ongoing Reading Journal	*Complete*

Acknowledgements

Thank you to Maggie de Vries, who helped me take this story from a five-minute writing assignment to a thesis and beyond. I certainly would have floundered without her encouragement, knowledge and guidance. I am grateful for Sandy Bogart Johnston, Erin Haggett and the team at Scholastic who were wonderfully patient and thorough throughout. Thank you to Aldo Fierro for an amazing book design, and to Simon Kwan for bringing Robbie's doodles to life.

Thank you to everyone in the MACL program at UBC who provided direction and expertise, including Linda Svendsen, Rhea Tregebov, Judith Saltman and Judy Brown. I thank Joanna Topor MacKenzie, Dorothea Wilson-Scorgie, Lara LeMoal, Alana Husband, Joe Sales, the Writers' Exchange (including Jennifer Macleod, Sarah Maitland and Cito Catston), as well as countless others whose feedback, enthusiasm, help and love is so appreciated; all of you I'd like to name here, but you'll just have to recognize that this shout-out is for you.

And of course, thanks to all of my family, comprised of hilarious, wonderful and creative people. In particular, my brothers Curtiss and Andrew for teaching me to never forget a good or embarrassing story; my parents Diane and Robert for creating a home of love, support, jokes and epic poems; and to my cousin Courtney, my first writing partner and kindred spirit: thank you.

WOULD THE **REAL**
STANLEY CARROT
PLEASE
STAND UP?

ROB STEVENS

Stanley 'Carrot' has never fitted in. He's got bright
ginger hair, he's not sporty like his adoptive family, and
he's definitely not cool. For years he's waited to hear
from his birth mother... and then, on his 13th
birthday, a card arrives.

Stan wants to show his mum what she's been missing –
but he's got a feeling he'd be more of a disappointment
than a wonderkid. What he needs is a stand-in Stan,
someone who is handsome, sporty
and God's Gift to Mothers. Things
are going to get seriously confusing.

Just who is the real Stanley Carrot?

'Touching and funny'
Julia Eccleshare, Lovereading

9781783442287   £6.99

REBECCA STEAD

**WINNER OF THE GUARDIAN CHILDREN'S FICTION PRIZE
AND SHORTLISTED FOR THE CARNEGIE MEDAL**

When Georges moves into a new apartment block
he meets Safer, a twelve-year-old self-appointed
spy. Soon Georges has become his spy recruit. His
first assignment? To track the mysterious Mr X,
who lives in the flat upstairs. But as Safer becomes
more demanding, Georges starts to wonder: what
is a game and what is a lie?
How far is too far to go for
your only friend?

'A joy to read' *Independent*

'Rebecca Stead makes
writing this well look easy'
Philip Ardagh, Guardian

9781849395427 £6.99 Paperback

A TALE DARK & GRIMM

ADAM GIDWITZ

Reader: beware!

Lurking within these covers are sorcerers with dark spells, hunters with deadly aim and a baker with an oven big enough to cook children in. But if you dare, pick up this book and find out the true story of Hansel and Gretel – the story behind (and beyond) the breadcrumbs, the edible house and the outwitted witch. Come on in. It may be frightening, it's certainly bloody, and it's definitely not for the faint of heart, but unlike those other fairy tales you know, this one is true.

'Gidwitz balances the grisly violence of the original Grimms' fairy tales with a wonderful sense of humour and narrative voice. Check it out!'
Rick Riordan

'*A Tale Dark & Grimm* holds up to multiple readings, like the classic I think it will turn out to be.'
New York Times

9781783440870 £6.99

WE ARE ALL MADE OF MOLECULES

A NOVEL BY SUSIN NIELSEN

Meet Stewart. He's geeky, gifted but socially clueless.
His mom has died and he misses her every day.

Meet Ashley. She's popular, cool but her grades are no good.
Her dad has come out and moved out – but not far enough.

Their worlds are about to collide: Stewart and his dad are
moving in with Ashley and her mom. Stewart is trying to be
89.9% happy about it even as he struggles to fit in at his new
school. But Ashley is 110% horrified and can't get used to her
totally awkward home. And things are
about to get a whole lot more mixed up
when these two very different people
attract the attention of school hunk
Jared . . .

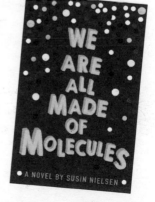

'Susin Nielsen is one of the best writers
working today' *Susan Juby*

9781783442324   Hardback £12.99